RIPPLES

AN ANTHOLOGY

BY

CLIFFORD L. CARTER

MARK FLEISHER

BELINDA BYNUM GREEN

J. KEITH JONES

VAL LOTZ

REGINA D' SCRIPTURA

GARY B. ZELINSKI

LIONHEART GROUP PUBLISHING
PUBLISHED IN THE USA

RIPPLES
AN ANTHOLOGY
JULY 2024 ~ FIRST EDITION

FOR INFORMATION REGARDING PERMISSION, EMAIL LIONHEART GROUP PUBLISHING: PERMISSIONS@LIONHEARTGROUPPUBLISHING.COM

COVER BY SANDRA MILLER

PAPERBACK ISBN: 978-1-938505-67-6
HARDBACK ISBN: 978-1-938505-68-3
LIBRARY OF CONGRESS CONTROL NUMBER: 2024941310

10 9 8 7 6 5 4 3 2 1

PUBLISHED BY LIONHEART GROUP PUBLISHING, LANDER, WYOMING, USA

PUBLISHED IN THE USA ~ ALL RIGHTS RESERVED.

VISIT US ON THE WEB AT WWW.LIONHEARTGROUPPUBLISHING.COM

LIONHEART GROUP PUBLISHING IS AN IMPRINT OF
LIONHEART GUILD, INC; A NON-PROFIT

DEDICATION

To those whose paths have intertwined with ours, shaping our journeys in ways seen and unseen.

This anthology is a testament to the intricate web of connections that bind us all, transforming our lives through shared moments, whispers of wisdom, and acts of kindness.

May these stories remind us of the profound impact we have on one another, and the beauty of our collective human experience.

Be kind.

RIPPLES

TABLE OF CONTENTS

POND CREEK

I was raised down on Pond Creek
On a dirt and muddy road,

In a house with more love
Than you could behold.

I can see my mom and dad
Working in the fields

From daylight to darkness On a
farm that wouldn't yield.

Dad and Mom are gone now
To heaven up above

But the memory of their happiness
Was a house full of love.

Now my sister and brothers
Have all gone out west

To a place called Oklahoma That
they all love the best.

But this old lonely Pond Creek
Keeps me back here

In the Wabash River bottoms
With my memories so clear.

C. Leroy Carter

1933-2002

INTRODUCTION

RIPPLES, AN ANTHOLOGY

IN THE INTRICATE TAPESTRY OF human existence, each thread is interwoven with countless others, creating patterns that are both beautiful and complex. This anthology delves into the profound and often unrecognized ways our actions, words, and even our mere presence can influence the lives of those around us.

From a simple smile exchanged with a stranger to the thoughtful advice given to a friend, every interaction holds the potential to create ripples that extend far beyond the moment. Our daily lives are a series of encounters and decisions that shape not only our own experiences but also the experiences of others, often in ways we may never fully comprehend.

Through a diverse collection of stories, essays, and reflections, this anthology explores the myriad ways in which our lives are interconnected. It highlights the power of kindness, the significance of empathy, and the impact of our choices on the world around us.

RIPPLES

Each piece serves as a reminder that, whether we are aware of it or not, we are constantly influencing the world and the people within it.

As you journey through these pages, may you be inspired to recognize the subtle yet powerful ways you affect those around you and to embrace the responsibility and opportunity to create positive ripples in your everyday life.

GARCIA Y VEGA

CLIFFORD L. CARTER

FOR YEARS, TAROT HAD BEEN a curiosity that moved me to darken the doorstep of many a card readers' lair. I was interested in the view expressed in the cards and how closely it matched (or not at all) to the intuitive way I found myself weaving through life from place to place allowing what I called, the Universe, to guide me.

About halfway between Coeur d'Alene, Idaho and the Canadian border lies the small town of Sandpoint—positioned alongside Lake Pend Oreille to the south and the Selkirk Mountain range to the north. What a magical place that had been to me, with towering Tamarack pines lining deep blue water.

My life became settled in that northern town thirty miles or so south of the Canadian border, hidden amongst trees. I was far and away from the life I had left behind, traveling from one place to another and yet another—being blown by the slightest draft that came along.

It seemed like that little cabin in the woods might hold on to me forever.

I imagined roots pushing deep in the ground, searching for water and sustenance—becoming more and more stable as I grew. Raising chicken, tending a garden, clearing only a few trees and scrub not to wake the neighbors of my existence. I relaxed into a routine of waking up with the rising sun and sleeping with the night sky.

Dreaming of what had been, imagining what would be, the tarot kept returning to my subconscious. Night after night, the tarot informed me of change, transformation, and when a restless time was near.

One of my good friends, Kelly, shared with me a tarot-reading class was forming in the weeks to come, and I might even find a flyer tacked to a pole near the church. Now, that friend was not ordinary. She was the very first person I ran into upon arriving to Sandpoint on a scouting mission—not sure if that place would be in my future or a much more usual move from east to west and then back to the east from the west, stopping only for a couple years in the north and south.

Traveling was my thing. *Gypsy* was a much more interesting way of describing myself. My parents believed I was running away from something I had not confronted or was not interested in dealing with. They were, of course, right. But nonetheless, I was being me, seeing the world for one reason or another.

Kelly told me straight to my face orange was my color—glancing upwards, as if searching for confirmation from her guides. She also told me about chakras and how the sacral (or second) chakra was the color orange. Once I transformed my inner work, the color orange would finally accept me.

Wasting no time, I found the flyer attached to a telephone pole near Sandpoint's First Lutheran Church and contacted the tarot teacher about her class. Excited about being able to see my own future without reaching out to every roadside psychic stand which always promised a bright financially stable secure married life with six kids.

I remember the church well because I was raised at Emmaus Lutheran Church in Dorsey, Illinois. Emmaus Lutheran was LCMS and First Lutheran was ELCA, meaning my childhood church sang tired old hymns from an outdated blue hymnal, and the other practiced meditation and yoga.

My tarot class met at what seemed to be an old, abandoned storage facility. Dimly lit, six chairs around a makeshift dining table. *How fitting*, I thought, *for a supernatural experience.*

Our first class covered working with a pendulum.

I was instructed one must sleep with the pointy-ended stone hanging from a chain (much like a plum bob) until the next class. So, it either tunes to your frequency or rejects you altogether. Spinning to the right for yes and left for no, the pendulum had the ability to verify any reading that might feel was going in the right or wrong direction.

Class two started by observing my technique of moving the pendulum (gifted to me by the teacher) only using my intention. A beautiful pink rose quartz, cadged in silver, hanging from a short chain with a bead attached to the opposite end. When placed between two fingers, it wouldn't slip through and still allow the pointed rose quartz to channel my energy, showing right or wrong. I had, of course, not read the preclass list of must-have ritualistic paraphernalia clearly written on the flyer.

In my defense, there were about six thousand nails left in that telephone pole from past events and happenings around town, with bits and pieces of yard sale signs still stuck into the cracks and crevasses.

"Give me a yes," I said, and the pendulum shifted from side to side, followed by a clockwise movement. "Give me a no," I said, and the pendulum slowly came to a halt and then spun counterclockwise.

"Looks good," my teacher said. "And now we can move on."

It was so challenging for me to memorize major arcana cards and their significance, along with the role they played in translating someone's past, present, and future. I quickly gave up on the task of memorization and moved to interpreting the images placed on each card.

Every tarot deck slightly differs. Those differences determine the illustration and how they might relate to the major and minor arcana.

Also, we were required to memorize the spreads. Meaning, the way the cards were placed on a table or flat-ish surface. Placing the cards vertical and horizontal, choosing from one to eight, telling our life story—beginning, middle, and end.

There were many different tarot spreads that could accurately communicate someone's inner true self, what had been getting in the way, struggles, hopes and dreams for the future, and an outcome based on the past.

I was using a borrowed *Rider Weight* tarot—the gold standard for beginners all the way to the pros. I had no attachment to the deck and went out searching for my own between class two and three.

My first stop was to see Kelly, my psychic friend who recommended the tarot class in the first place. She worked at a little metaphysical shop in town that had a nice selection of cards. Remembering my life work had been with the color orange, along with the chakra associated, combined with my parent telling me I was running from something I did not want to face, I spotted an orange box with *Inner Child Cards* written on the cover, adorned with a fairy riding a giant lunar moth.

Yep, that was the one. Especially since I checked it out with my pendulum—spinning clockwise, validating my choice.

Class three and still unable to memorize the course work, I simply followed along. I stumbled through the instructor's use of the major and minor arcana as well as the different spreads. Then, we were put into pairs and instructed to take a crack at reading each other's cards.

I asked my partner to shuffle while focusing on them. When they were confident connecting to the tarot, place them on the table—breaking the deck into three piles with their left hand and putting the deck back together.

I placed the cards face down, in order from one to eight without looking at the cards as they went from hand to table. Then I check the spread with my pendulum, asking if that was an accurate reading for the person sitting in front of me.

The pendulum spun clockwise, giving me a yes.

As the reading continued, my body felt cold and the hair on my arms and legs stood straight up. I was afraid to tell this person what I was thinking or feeling for fear I might be wrong and look like a fake or fraud guessing my way through the reading.

Throwing caution to the wind, mouth open, I said the first thing that came out, only pausing to take a breath.

At one point, I stopped as my mind spun faster and faster until I could hear myself talking but not so sure what I was even saying. It seemed like the room felt similar and different at the same time. I experienced a feeling of floating, rising out of my body without the ability to pull myself back down into the chair.

The next thing I remember was the teacher placing her hand on my shoulder, asking how the reading was going. At that point, all the out-of-body experiences came to a screeching halt. I was back in the chair, fellow student sitting across from me with her eyes as big as the moon.

I asked what was wrong.

She told me what I had said to her was so accurate that it was impossible for me to know any those things.

"Sharing my past had been so shameful that I simply bottled it up never to revisit again. Your insight from a slightly different perspective enabled me to expand my consciousness past the obstacles that have been holding me back."

Now my eyes were as large as the moon. I confessed I could not remember what I had said.

"I'm truly sorry if I offended you in any way with my words and hope they are somehow helpful in moving you past any stuck points you might be experiencing."

It was then my turn to get a reading from a fellow student.

The person I read refused to read my cards. She said she was scared of what might happen. She was not prepared for something unexpected, as I might levitate or even something more outrageous could happen.

The teacher said she would pair with me and had the experience to manage most anything that might take place, short of my head spinning in circles. She then laughed uncontrollably.

"Shuffle the cards," she said, "And place them on the table. Cut the cards into three stacks and then put the stacks back together using your left hand."

She placed the cards in the same spread I had used for the previous reading, from one to eight. She did not ask her pendulum if the reading was accurate. She closed her eyes for a moment. I'm guessing she was grounding herself. She had not discussed that aspect, nor did she discuss shielding oneself from the person being read. That came in a later class on how to protect oneself from any negative energy that might come our way.

She turned the cards right side up, as she explained the meaning of each card. My job was to verify if the reading was on track. She spoke about my true nature and what was standing in the way of fully embracing the who I really am. She shared events that were close to me in a general way and pointed to struggles as well.

That time, my body became very hot and I felt beads of sweat running down my back between my shoulders. I had chills at the same time, along with the hairs on my arms and legs raising up like the fuzzy hairs on a freshly picked peach.

It was then my turn to ask a question.

"As you were speaking to me, all I could think about was my grandmother. I thought that was odd because my grandmother passed away more than ten years ago."

As a child, I remembered, my mother and my grandmother's heated conversations boiling over our black plastic phone attached to the wall near the basement with a thirty-foot twisty cord. It seemed like every night Grandma would call. Mother directly sent me off to bed. I intently listened to their voices getting louder with every step closer to my bedroom door.

Once in bed, I saw the living room light cast shadows of mother pacing back and forth, as if she were floating like a hot-air balloon being tethered by that twisty black phone cord.

She frequently knocked on the door saying, "You had better be in bed when I come back here."

Those nightly conversations printed a childhood image of my grandmother not being a good person, and yet every time I got to see her, I was so excited. Excited to play in the giant house she lived in all by herself, with an attic that had doorways as tall as a six-year-old boy. My favorite place to explore and hide for hours was in those attic dormers, searching for what treasure Grandma had hidden in that dark dusty place.

When grandma passed, I was living in Kansas City working in a retail store called *Chess King*. I decided to come home for her funeral, not fully realizing what she had meant to me. On the drive over, I remembered all those adventures in that giant house with little attic doorways, leading to magical places filled with treasure.

I remembered the *Ouija* board my cousins and I played with at family reunions, asking it all kinds of question with each of use. Placing two fingers on the planchette as it effortlessly moved from letter to letter—demonstrating our collective psychic abilities by channeling intention into our fingertips.

All those memories flooded my brain as the teacher shared what she had seen in my reading. I floated away to the past, not really listening to her.

But, there had been an opening in my mind that took me to another place in time.

She was in mid-sentence when I blurted out, "I think my grandmother read tarot cards."

Oh my God. It must be true. How would I know this? Because of the **Ouija** *board?* I asked myself. I kept thinking over and over again, *My grandmother was a tarot reader, and now I am in a class learning the craft just as she had done many years before me.*

It was really all speculation and the only way to know for sure was to speak to my mother and hope it was a good day to bring up the subject.

I called mother that very evening, unable to wait a moment longer. I prefaced the conversation with, "I would like to ask you a question about Grandmother, but first I want to tell you about a class I am taking in Sandpoint, Idaho."

She gasped and said, "You had not told me you were living in Sandpoint." Last she knew, I was in a town called Pocatello.

Once we navigated through my Sandpoint, Idaho secret, I recounted the tarot class I was attending, in addition to other interesting experiences I had along the way.

The whole time, mother was silent—except for an occasional, "Uh-huh, uh-huh."

Once I finished talking about the class, it was time for my question. I said to my mother in a hesitant voice, "I am curious if grandmother might have been interested in tarot? I had this idea, thought, premonition... Just something that was telling me that grandmother was interested in tarot in some way."

Mother replied, "You could not have known about that because it was one of the biggest shameful secrets the family kept hidden. The answer is 'yes'. Of course she knew about tarot."

The moment she said I couldn't have known, I could see mother's eyes rolling around in her head—not certain how she would proceed without an out-and-out lie.

"Your grandmother, Vircil Telkamp, in the 1940s borrowed a plumber's van from her eldest son, Gene, and drove it to Granite City, Illinois—about a half an hour from our home, to consort with a very well-known African-American tarot reader... And do who knows what else. It was so shameful to the family and our neighbors... She sped home hours later with two incense sticks and a fruit jar full of disgusting tea. Or, that's what she said it was. I and my four siblings vowed never to go near that fruit jar filled with 'tea'."

Mother went on to share Vircil (her mother) took her to a couple's home in St Louis, Missouri when I was very young. They left me alone with a woman, while grandma went to the basement with a mysterious man, only to appear hours later. Mother even told me that she herself went to a woman in Granite City with a few co-workers from the *Owen's Illinois Glass Factory* to get a reading. The reader refused to speak to one of my mother's friends after confiding in my mother that the woman would have some very bad troubles in a month, or so.

That woman was in a fatal car crash one month and one day after the reader refused to speak to her.

Madam Tunningly was a well-respected tarot/fortune teller who foretold a great flood in Alton,

Illinois in the early 1950s, along with stunningly accurate forecasts of the rise and fall of prominent local figures, affairs, and such in the area. So, when Madam Tunningly proclaimed the future, one had better listen.

I only wish I had known that side of Grandmother when I was growing up. I remember Mother fighting with my grandmother most of the time, and my grandma holding my big toe and calling me 'Ninny' as a child.

Even though I previously said I had only one question, I then had another, considering the facts Mother had relayed.

My question was, "I wonder if she had cards and if so, what happened to them?"

Considering in the past, every ask of my mother was met with a 'no' before the ask fully left my lips, I was kind of trembling on the other end of the phone.

She said, "Of course Grandma had cards. I have them in the cigar tin she kept them in."

My heart raced as I formed my next and final question.

"I would love to have her cards. I know how much they mean to you, and I promise to take good care of them. If you ever want them back, you can be sure I will send them directly to you—even using overnight federal express if that would make you feel better. May I have them?"

Then, I took a deep breath and held it.

After a few moments, Mother replied. She claimed she would need to think hard on the subject—not to encourage me to engage in tarot reading, just like Grandma had.

"Regardless of the long-kept secret, I still cannot imagine how you knew about this," she said. "Did you talk to Aunt Dorthy about this subject? Because I can call and ask her right now. You know she will tell me the truth. And, if you did and if she told you, then that's it. I'm done with her interfering with my life as she always does."

"No. I promise. I did not ask Dorthy. I called you right away, in fact. My class finished only hours ago."

"Well... Let me think about it. I will let you know when I decide what to do."

When I crawled into bed that night, pulling the sheets and blankets over my head, I did something I had never done before. I asked Grandma if she would talk to Mother and ask her to give me her tarot cards.

A fog appeared in my mind's eyes with purple and white, pushing each color back and forth, dancing behind my eyelids.

I thought, *Wow! Maybe this is my grandmother letting me know she is here, and she is listening.*

I woke up the next morning to my mother's phone call. I can honestly say she never calls me. I figured Grandma spoke to her while she was sleeping.

Mother called to tell me she and Dad were taking another road trip and would not be near a phone for about two weeks.

"Here is another little thing I will tell you, and don't let it go to your head. Okay? Your grandmother told me when you were born that she had marked you. She did this because she already knew even before you were born that you were going to be special. This had been the brunt of our arguments all those years on how I would raise you, as I was determined to keep her out at all cost. And, now look what happened. You found out anyway."

A couple weeks later, after Mother had returned from her trip, she called again. That was two phone calls in just over two weeks. Either the sky was falling, or she was visited by Vircil Telkamp from the grave and beyond.

I'm not really sure yet the proper terminology to use when someone has been dead and gone for years. I mean, when those dead and not gone contacts someone who is living.

Mother said, in a frustrated voice, "I've given up on any idea that I, myself, have a choice in the matter. All I could think about on our trip were those damn cards. We went to the Grand Canyon after passing by Pikes Peak and the Royal Gorge. Traveled to Reno, Nevada on a dusty dirt road. Getting lost before I even got a chance at the slots.

"Every time I pulled that handle, watching those barrels spin 'round and around, all I saw was your face and Mother's face flashing over and over and over. Every time I closed my eyes to sleep, and when

I got a chance to look out the window, all I saw was your grandmother smiling back at me saying, 'See? I told you so'."

She continued. "I have decided to send you all her cards, packed inside the safety of that cigar tin. Please do me a favor and if you ever decide you don't want them, send them back to me for safe keeping."

I agreed.

I patiently waited for Grandmother's cards to arrive. I also shared with my tarot class about my grandmother and all the twists and turns, talking to my mother through my late grandmother, and how I was going to acquire her special cards.

Days passed with my anticipation of Grandma's cards getting the best of me every time I walked down that muddy path to get the mail. After a week, there they were—in a box the size of a two-square toaster. A little beat up on its journey to my home outside Sandpoint, Idaho.

Carefully cutting the tape not to damage any-thing hidden beneath cardboard, I pulled out pages of crinkled *Alton Telegraph*.

There it was. *Garcia y Vega* cigars painted clear as can be on top of a dented tin with rusty spots, pealing from the top and bottom edges.

The lid held fast to the contents, when I attempted to open it. On observation, I found not only several tarot decks inside, there were also postcards from Grandma's travels that had yet to be mailed from Milwaukee, Wisconsin's *Hotel Medford*, along with

a sight-seeing miniature spiral-bound booklet—
Home of the Braves stamped on the cover.

A white envelope, folded in such a way to protect
its contents of what looked to be a newspaper article
scotch taped together, explained the various layouts
of *Madame Signa Mystic* fortune telling cards. Also,
a brand-new never-used deck of said cards, alongside a well-worn tarot deck—complete with lipstick
stains on the *Wish* and *Marriage* cards.

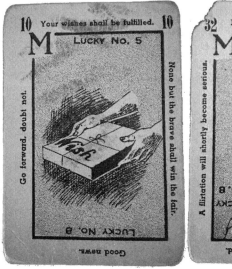

What appeared to be a regular deck of playing
cards was tightly bound with their meanings written
on the edges of each card, enabling a novice reader,
like myself, to accomplish an accurate reading.

More than thirty years later, I still have my
grandmother's cards kept in that dented *Garcia y
Vega* cigar tin, now with a few more creases and
wrinkles.

I have been reading tarot and using my grandmother's precious cards on special occasions, when I need a little extra help. I use them along with the same pendulum gifted to me by my very first tarot teacher. I gave the *Inner Child* tarot deck to a couch-surfer friend who seemed like his work was with the color orange, along with childhood obstacles getting in his way of fully embracing self.

It is truly magical that my grandmother marked me before I was born. And even though her children kept that secret for so many years, she finally saw to it that her *Garcia y Vega* cigar tin, full of Grandma's tears, joys, loves, and losses, made its way to the very person destined to have it.

Still, I speak to Grandmother.

And now, I speak to my mother (who has since passed away) every time I come across Grandma's *Garcia y Vega* cigar tin.

ABOUT THE AUTHOR

CLIFFORD L. CARTER

CLIFFORD CARTER HAS ALWAYS BEEN a writer, if only by dreaming of the day he would actualize one single thought placed on a page to be reviewed and marveled at—ever evolving into a style driven by his intuitive nature exploring the world.

Writing has been a way for Clifford to express his feelings onto the page, as they flow in and out of his consciousness, like a river winding through a deep canyon—eventually reaching the sea. With every rock outcropping, another twist and turn surfaces from the dark murky waters of life experience.

Clifford's family, and growing up in a tiny mid-western town, offered a box or vessel-like container that enabled him to turn inward to the safety of his own thoughts. It took a literal tricennial to accomplish his first piece, which became an award-winning mindfulness curriculum followed by a meditation manual.

RIPPLES

FLOWERS FROM ANNIE

MARK FLEISHER

FOR A BRIEF TIME SEVERAL years ago, I worked in Chicago. When my day ended, I took a city bus to a stop a few blocks from the cramped apartment I could barely afford. On my walk home, I passed a flower shop owned by a young woman named Annie. I knew her name, because the letters were stenciled in bright red on the store window.

Though my bank account was meager, and my wallet almost never carried spare bills, I stopped every two or three days and bought a modest flower. Not because I loved or even liked flowers, nor did I know anything about them. Admittedly, I couldn't tell a tiger lily from a hibiscus even if threatened with physical punishment.

No, I'd stint on a necessity to buy a blossom because I was plain and not-so-simply attracted to Annie.

I was too shy and too poor for any outward expression of feelings. *Surely*, I believed, *any number of suitors would be drawn to her lovely face, shoulder-length chestnut hair, winning smile, and other all-too-obvious features.*

One fall day, I decided to utter more than the few words I usually mustered.

"I'm kind of new to Chicago," I said. "Wondering how long you've had this shop?"

She explained she'd been running the shop for about two years. "My mom's parents—my grandparents—had the shop for years. They retired and moved to Florida to get away from Chicago winters. My parents had relocated to the West Coast. My grandparents wanted to keep the shop in the family. My brother and I are the only grandkids, and he wasn't interested. So, I was it."

"Probably not what you planned?"

"For sure, but I'm happy it turned out this way. I had a business degree from the University of Illinois and landed a job in a small-town bank after graduation.

"After a while, I realized small-town life was not for me, so I came back to Chicago and started job hunting. I joined a brokerage firm as a researcher. Kind of interesting at first, writing reports about companies.

"One day, after sitting at a computer for eight hours, I came to the conclusion the job felt cold, uninspiring. I had virtually no contact with people, and I always considered myself a people person."

I mentally kicked myself in the head, realizing what an idiot I was. "Can I interrupt for a minute? I feel like a fool. I was so interested in your story, I never told you my name. It's Dan, Dan Fleming. Everyone calls me Danny, but I prefer Dan. Makes me seem more mature. At least, I think so.

"So, you left the brokerage job and then what?"

Annie told me when her mom and dad left Chicago, she didn't want to see the shop close. Her parents couldn't find a buyer, so she decided to get out of the corporate rat race and give the flower shop a try for a couple of years.

"I wasn't a total newcomer. I had worked in the shop after school and then summers when I was in college. It's kind of a neighborhood institution, and I got a lot of support from loyal customers and other businesses in the area.

"I'm sorry. I've rattled on for way too long and probably bored you to death. Besides, I'd like to hear about you, Dan. Look, the shop is closed Sundays, so how about we meet for breakfast? By the way, it's Yates."

"Yates?"

"My last name.

"There's a little hole-in-the-wall place that's been in business, gosh, since I was a kid. Great omelets. Not far from here on East Washington. How's nine o'clock sound?"

"Terrific."

I could not sleep much Saturday, lying awake thinking of our breakfast date. Okay, I admitted, not really a date, but at least a chance to be with her even if it was only for an hour or so.

I found the 'hole in the wall' and arrived ten minutes early.

The place was pretty crowded. I asked a server if I could grab a table until my friend arrived.

She said, "No problem, sit where you want."

There were two empty tables in a small alcove, and I sat down at one.

Annie arrived shortly thereafter. I waved to her. As she strode toward the table, I stood up and pulled out a chair for her.

Ever the gentleman, I thought, because my mom and dad had taught me well.

Annie wore jeans and an Illinois sweatshirt. She had her hair pulled back in a ponytail.

I remembered back in senior year of high school I had a crush on a girl with a ponytail. Nothing came of it after I found out she was pretty serious with a guy in college.

Our server left menus on the table, and when she returned she asked if we were ready to order.

I beckoned to Annie. She ordered a vegetable omelet. My choice was a Western omelet. We both asked for coffee.

"Okay, Dan. You're on," she said, handing me an imaginary microphone.

"Not very exciting, but here goes. I grew up in Ohio. My dad worked in a factory, my mom took care of the house. I did okay in school, nothing spectacular. I wrote sports articles for the school paper and got the idea I wanted to be a writer.

"I went to a state school, majored in English, and took a few creative-writing courses. During summers, my dad got me work in the factory. Boring work—taking auto parts off shelves, and boxing them up for shipping. But the money wasn't bad.

"After graduation, I thought I'd like to go to New York or maybe San Francisco and write. Of course, I had no idea what it cost to live in those places. I was kind of dreamy.

"One day, my parents sat me down and said, 'You'd better get a real job if you want to be on your own.'

"A woman I knew in college—she was a year ahead of me—worked in a publishing house here in Chicago. She said they were hiring editorial assistants. So, I applied, not even knowing what an editorial assistant did. They must have been hard up because they hired me."

Our scrumptious-looking omelets arrived just as Annie asked what my work involved.

Silently apologizing to my mom for talking with my mouth full, I strove to give Annie an abridged answer to her question.

"Well, work with editors to manage publication schedules, attend meetings with writers and agents, proofread manuscripts, checking facts, adding my two cents about layout and design, Basically provide info for the higher-ups who make the decisions."

"Are you writing at all?"

"A few ideas floating around in my head and some scribbles in a notebook. Nothing actually done, but that's one of my goals. Maybe I'll make a New Year's resolution to get off my butt and finish something."

We polished off our breakfasts. Our server cleared the empty plates and placed the bill in front of me.

I reached for my wallet, but Annie scooped up the check, saying she invited me so it's only fair she paid.

"Thanks, Annie, maybe we could do this next Sunday, and it'll be my treat."

"I'd love to, but there's a family wedding in Springfield. And the week after, my college roommate is getting married. I'm the maid of honor plus taking care of all the flowers. And I'll be in Milwaukee over Thanksgiving with my brother and his family."

If anything, I am persistent. I asked if maybe the Sunday after the Thanksgiving weekend might work.

"Afraid not." Annie said she was closing the shop for ten days or so and planning a vacation before the Christmas rush began.

"Where to?"

"Maybe Aruba. I need sun. You been?"

"Nope. Hey, it's your day off and I'm sure you've got lots to do. Take good care and thanks again for breakfast. It was really good."

Annie nodded, gently hugged me, and told me to be well.

We went our separate ways.

I was busy at work, racking up lots of over-time. Then, Thanksgiving in Ohio followed by an unexpected turn of events. I didn't see Annie until the second week in January, when I walked by the shop.

She waved and motioned me to come in.

"Hey stranger, how are you? You look tired. Working hard?"

"Yeah, that, and my mom had an accident. Slipped on the ice right after Thanksgiving. Broke her leg and ankle. Had surgery and she's been in rehab for a month. My dad is taking it hard. I took vacation time and trying to get back to Ohio on weekends to help him cope with everything."

Annie expressed her concern and when she put a comforting hand on mine, I couldn't help but notice the diamond ring.

"Is that an engagement ring?" I asked, knowing full well it was. "Who's the lucky guy?"

"Remember I said I was in my roommate's wedding? Well, Ben was there. We had dated in school, and it got serious. But after graduation I stayed in Illinois, and he got a great job working for a civil engineering company in South America. We agreed that a very long-distance relationship wouldn't work."

Annie's roommate had not told her or Ben of each other's attendance at the wedding.

"She didn't know how either of us would react. I was flabbergasted to see him again. I think he felt the same way. Anyway, he said he'd love to catch up. But the wedding was pretty noisy, so we agreed to get together in Chicago a few days after."

A customer interrupted Annie's monologue.

Just as well, I thought. I really didn't need— or want—to hear all the details, but I wasn't about to say so.

"Anyway, we went out five or six nights straight and I could sense those old feelings returning. A few weeks later, he had to go out of town for three days and we talked on the phone each night. When Ben got back, he surprised the heck out of me and asked me to marry him."

I offered my congratulations, hoping my disappointment didn't obscure my sincerity.

"So, when's the wedding?"

"Late summer, early fall. Depends on a few things. By the way, consider yourself invited."

"Thanks. Doesn't Ben have to go back to South America? What about the flower shop after the wedding?" I had more questions but thought I'd keep my mouth shut.

"Actually, no. Ben decided four years of building roads and bridges in the jungle was enough. He made great money and saved a bundle, so he has the luxury of taking his time lining up another job. The flower shop? I guess it depends where we'll be."

"Hey, I've got some errands to run. Congratulations again, and I wish you much happiness."

I didn't see Annie much in the following months. I was promoted to assistant editor and, while I enjoyed a fatter paycheck, my days were more intense and much longer.

I went by the flower shop one Saturday and saw another woman behind the counter. She told me she'd been hired to manage the business, although Annie stopped in one or two days a week.

My higher pay allowed me to buy a wedding present for Annie—silver candlesticks. When the wedding invitation arrived, I debated whether or not to go. As much as it might hurt, I thought it might be the last time I saw her, especially if she and Ben moved away.

I went to the ceremony but skipped the reception for reasons... Well, you can figure out.

I remembered hearing an old Frank Sinatra tune, *I Fall in Love Too Easily* and thought it should be my anthem.

On my walks around the neighborhood, I made sure to avoid the flower shop. What was the point? Whatever connection we may have had was pretty much unplugged. Why inflict more pain on my wounded heart?

My fortunes eventually improved, taking me to a new and better job in Boston—far from the flower shop and its beguiling owner.

Business took me back to Chicago a few years later. For old time's sake, I longed to see Annie again. I knew her still owning the flower shop was a long shot. But, what the hell?

I thought about taking the bus but decided my new stature would let me spring for a twenty-dollar cab ride (plus generous tip) from my hotel in the Loop. My chatty Eritrean driver dropped me at what I was sure was the correct address. But no *Annie* stenciled on the storefront window, no flowers in sight, and certainly no sign of the woman I silently loved years ago.

In the flower shop's place was what we called back in the day a variety store—kind of a scaled-down *Five and Dime* offering an olio of items, many of them unnecessary for daily life.

Maybe I had the wrong address. So, I turned up the collar of my overcoat for protection against those Chicago winds and walked to the nearby corner. I found what in my heart I knew I would find—the intersection jibed with my memory.

I walked back to the variety store, found the owner, and asked if Annie had relocated to another part of town or closed the shop after she married.

I was rocked by what he told me.

Annie had passed away from an incurable condition. What, he didn't know. The fellow from whom she rented the space had found a new tenant in the variety store owner.

Knowing I couldn't deal with another talkative cab driver, I walked back to the hotel, passing several bars. Each one tempted me to drop in and down a strong drink to warm my body and ease the sorrow I felt.

Figuring my hotel room a safer choice, I opened the mini-bar and found a bottle of *Jack Daniel's*—about the size they serve on airplanes. I drank it straight in one gulp.

Bone tired and emotionally wasted, I crawled into the king bed, hoping Mr. Daniel would help put me out. He did.

I awoke at some point in the middle of the night—at least, I think I did. Before me stood Annie, clutching a flower in each hand. One blossom was bright orange, the other lemon yellow.

"This is a tiger lily," Annie said, extending the orange flower. "And this a hibiscus. Now, you can tell the difference between them."

She added, before her ghostly form faded into the surrounding ethereal light, "By the way, I liked you a lot."

I flew home to Boston two days later. I passed the two-hour flight time at 35,000 feet, finishing the in-flight magazine crossword puzzle, dozing a bit, and exchanging a frequent flyer drink ticket for a Jack and *Coke*.

Carol met me at Logan International. I kissed her a little harder than usual, hugged her a few seconds longer than normal, and said I missed her a lot.

I meant it.

"I missed you, too. Did the meetings in Chicago go well?" Carol asked, as we navigated through rush hour traffic on the forty-five-minute drive to our home in Waltham.

"Fine," I said. "Just fine."

RIPPLES

ABOUT THE AUTHOR

MARK FLEISHER

BORN IN BROOKLYN, NEW YORK, and now living in Albuquerque, New Mexico, Mark Fleisher's most recent and fifth book—*Knowing When*—was a finalist for the 2023 Best New Mexico Book of Poetry.

His poetry and prose work have appeared in numerous print and online publications in the United States, Canada, United Kingdom, Kenya, Nigeria and India.

He earned a journalism degree from Ohio University and then served in the United States Air Force, lastly as a combat news reporter in Vietnam.

Following his military service, Mark held writing and editing positions at upstate New York and Washington, D.C. newspapers before embarking on a freelance writing career.

RIPPLES

FULL MOON MADNESS

BeLinda Bynum Green

I STARTED WRITING AGAIN WITH THE approach of the full moon. I don't know if it had chased my demons away or brought them to be my muse.

Life these past few days had been very strange. I had allowed myself to indulge in everything I usually imbibed in moderation or not at all. There had been late-night dinners of bread and pasta with red wine, followed by the most decadent of desserts and then dancing for hours.

My body refused to leave the bed in the mornings to follow my daily routine of going to the gym at 5AM. The unusually late hours I had begun keeping of course did not help.

I'd even met a very charming young man at the *Rose Bar* in the *Delano Hotel* and took him straight to his bed. It was quite unlike me in many, many moons. But this full moon was different somehow, and its waxing had swept along with it my total abandonment to conservatism as I'd known it.

Driving and looking up at this moon that was near enough to touch, I wanted to shred my clothing off, throw my head back, and howl at it. Speeding along with the window down and my hair blowing in the wind, I felt like a mad woman—possessed by a spirit that was not my own.

The hair on my arm stood on end. The night was warm but chill bumps covered my body.

Most of my skin was exposed with the new fashion I had fancied of late. Short exotic sundresses that showed miles of my long legs and a gratuitous view of cleavage had become my uniform.

I bought ten sundresses on my last trip to Cancun, only because the prints were so beautiful. They reminded me of sunrises, sunsets, flower gardens, and dancing flames. I had intended to have the dresses made into a type of collage tapestry to cover one of the walls in my home.

Now they adorned my body, making me feel like a goddess.

And a goddess is now what I've become. But what good is a goddess with nothing to wield her power over. I felt powerful—like anything, or anyone, would be mine if I so desired. I tapped my long red fingernails on the steering wheel, feeling my mind race in a thousand different directions. I'd never worn red fingernail polish in my life. I looked into my rear-view mirror and blew a kiss. I seductively licked my ruby red lips and turned myself on in the process.

If it were not for the familiar brown eyes that never changed, looking back, I don't think I would have recognized myself at all. They were sensual, serious, comedic, accusing, and icy all at the same time. Only my facial expression changed.

Most people never knew how to take me when there was not a smile on my face.

Words drenched in sugar could be flowing from my lips, but the absence of my smile made the words seem counterfeit. I rarely smiled and usually allowed myself to do so as a reward to someone who had no idea where they stood with me.

I was not mean by nature. Smiles just did not come easily to my lips, even if I were in the best of moods.

"Life is a photographer, but I refuse to smile for the camera." Somewhere along the way, I had made that line up to apply to myself.

I drove men crazy with a sex appeal that smoldered under a Victorian-like demeanor. On the rare occasions I wore low-cut blouses, men were drawn to me by the hint of full bosoms.

Their lusts were somehow conflicted as the silver cross that hung between my breasts glared back at them with the threat of being smacked across the knuckles by Sister Agnes. I loved the dichotomy. The innocent vixen, I was.

But now, I was just a vixen. Come to think of it, no one who knew me had seen me since this transformation. They probably would have had me committed or exorcised. I laughed at the thought of my dearest friend seeing me this way.

I raced on into the night. Heaven help the officer if one should stop me now. He or she would definitely go away feeling as if he or she had been sensually violated somehow, without even being touched. I was in the mood to purr and raise temperatures.

I didn't know where I was going yet. Someone else was driving, hiding behind my mind's eye. I ended up at the *Eden Roc Hotel*. I valeted my car. The young man who came up to escort me out of my car got an eyeful of thigh as I put one leg out and then paused in the mirror to check my makeup.

I seductively looked up at him and said, "Please treat it right."

I dropped my gaze, almost batting my lashes like a starlet and exited my vehicle like a cat—ignoring his outstretched hand. Surely my skin would have burned him had he touched me.

I gazed up at the moon, which seemed to be right above me, and then walked up the steps. Every head turned to watch the self-possessed woman enter the lobby and walk towards the bar like she owned the place.

I ordered a raspberry vodka and orange juice and slid onto a chair at the bar. I felt the eyes on me, and suddenly spun around to face my voyeurs with a half-smile on my lips.

The women immediately dropped their gazes, some blushing, but the men were like a deer in headlights—they could not look away.

I turned back around to sip my drink, very pleased with the attention.

Twenty minutes later, I was bored, and my glass was empty. I declined the $250 bottle of *Veuve Clicquot Rosé* that had been sent over by an admirer. Two ladies sitting to my right were talking about a CEO's wedding taking place at the hotel.

I've always wanted to crash a wedding. It was on my bucket list.

I slid out of my seat and confidently walked across the lobby. I cajoled my way into the Mona Lisa Ballroom.

The wedding reception was pure opulence. The dance floor was packed, and I spotted the red-haired bride flitting from guest to guest for a quickie dance with each. Her cheeks were flushed as she was obviously feeling her champagne. Bottles of *Dom* were on every table. *Melt With You* by Modern English was playing.

I made my way to the middle of the dance floor near the bride and started my own little groove. Then, she spun from the arms of an older gentleman, and I grabbed her and did a half circle two-step as she giggled. On impulse, I dipped her and smiling, placed the gentlest kiss on her lips, leaving just a tiny bit of my red lipstick on her mouth.

I brought the bride back up, steadied her and disappeared into the crowd—leaving behind gasps from the guest who had been close enough to see the kiss.

Naughty me. I had kissed a girl.

There, number twelve and number seventeen had been knocked off my bucket list in one night.

I made my way out the lobby doors and retrieved my car.

I drove to Ocean Drive and found a parking spot off 11th Street. I slipped out of my *Choos,* walked barefoot over to the beach, and commandeered a lifeguard stand.

I sat there for the rest of the night, reflecting on the last few days leading up to the gorgeous full moon overhead. Then, the sun started rising on a cloudless horizon.

And as suddenly as it had come, I felt the lunar pull leaving my body. Thank goodness there would be no familiar witnesses to my days of debauchery. I was back to just plain old me. It was time to return my friends' calls that had filled up my voicemail.

I stood up and blew a kiss to the sun and made my way down the street. There was a Belgian Waffle with my name on it at the *News Café*.

At home, I busied myself fine tuning a proposal for work that had been given to me without much notice.

My company was courting the largest logistics company in Miami for a joint venture. I was suddenly the pitch woman when the CFO, after floundering for a month with pinning down a date, decided to inform us on Thursday he would be available for a meeting on the next Wednesday or in six weeks. We jumped on next Wednesday.

I had already been working from home since that Monday. So, I locked myself inside for the rest of the weekend through Tuesday, making graphs look innovative and interesting.

Wednesday morning, I showed up for the meeting exactly seven minutes late. I had always prided myself on being on time or early, but you can't control the gridlock from a roll-over accident on I-95.

Flustered, I glanced into the conference room through the gold framed glass. I didn't see the CFO for *Phoenix Logistics*.

My secretary came up and told me there had been a changing of the guard, and the new CEO wanted to attend in person with the support staff.

Great, just great, I thought to myself.

I walked in with my chin up, tossed out an apology for my tardiness, and went straight into my welcome from my notes.

A couple of people were straggling back to the table with coffee in hand. I paused as they were seated and looked up as the new CEO was being introduced to me.

My mouth opened to spout some canned pleasantry, and then I froze.

The CEO's cheeks turned almost as red as her hair. It was the bride fresh off her four-day honeymoon in Aruba.

I quickly recovered my face and walked over. Only our eyes were smiling and locked on each other, sharing a crimson-stained secret. I shook her hand, welcomed her, returned to the podium, and started flipping through the first of three dozen charts and graphs.

THE KISS

BELINDA BYNUM GREEN

Sitting in the shade waiting to be inspired,

Nothing's moved me since your kiss.

Funny how thirty seconds changes your life.

My eyes were closed, I was holding my breath.

When they opened, I saw a whole new world,

With possibilities of marriage,
children, a Volvo station wagon.

I've never wanted kids before.

Before you kissed me

I'm the international traveler,
lover, wanderer...

I leave men behind and fly away
to cities with leaning towers.

Flipped the script from Uncle Sam's men
flying away from me to Fiji, Guam, and Alaska

Well now, I'll send you a postcard, Sweetie.

I'll be back when Paris gets old.

Couldn't tame this shrew with
promises of the American dream,

White picket fences. A big house in suburbia.

But one kiss at exactly the right
moment from exactly the right man

Made me want to bake, wax floors
and paint the nursery blue.

The kiss that melted my passports, diner's
club cards, and Euro Rail passes,

Stopped the glamorous life dead in its tracks.

Yeah, I'll be your lady.

I promise to stick around for Thanksgiving,
Christmas, New Year's Eve,

To meet your mom, your sister,
your favorite niece.

You just don't know what you mean to me.

I'll give up the whole world just for your kiss.

ABOUT THE AUTHOR

BeLinda Bynum Green

For the last nineteen years, BeLinda Bynum Green has been married to the man of her dreams. She is a homeschooling mother of three children, living in South Florida. Writing has always been BeLinda's passion, followed by fitness and herbalism. She loves the beach, travel and exploring new adventures with her family.

As a Certified Personal Trainer and Life and Health Coach, BeLinda is dedicated to helping others achieve the best quality of life possible. She feels her strength and her weakness is that she's often working on writing multiple books at the same time.

BeLinda has many unpublished works that she plans to release in the near future. She believes she is the poster child for "there aren't enough hours in the day".

Her first self-published book is a book of poetry, *Raven's Flight.*

RIPPLES

On a Lonely Stretch of Road

J. Keith Jones

WHAT JUST HAPPENED? BETWEEN THE ringing, each beat of my heart thundered inside my ears. So much blood... soaking my carpet, running down the side of my face, and coating the man lying in my entryway.

Callie stood there, her eyes darting from the prone body to me, then back. I was in shock, I had to be. I opened my mouth, searching for a question, but nothing came out. I was still on my knees and sank back on my heels. *What now?* I covered my face with my hands.

What indeed.

The evening had been magical, wine, candle-light, and Bob Seger on the stereo.

* * *

Callie had wandered into the bar I frequented on the corner a couple of streets away just a few weeks ago. The shape of her body, face, lips...

everything, grabbed me immediately. I was riveted. There was one problem, I was painfully shy. She was the kind of woman I dreamed of, mooned over, but never approached.

She caught my stare. I averted my gaze and tried to play it cool. I glanced back and she grinned mildly, lips slightly parted, one eyebrow twitched recognition that I was looking again.

I realized that was my opening, but I knew it wasn't going to happen. It couldn't... I couldn't... It didn't matter. I didn't have to.

She waltzed right up to me, sat down, fixed me with those eyes, and said, "Hello stranger."

A couple of hours later, we were at my place.

The weeks since had been an unbelievable ride. I had never known a woman that direct.

* * *

I looked up, she was shaking me by the shoulders. The body still lay on the floor beside me. I think she was shouting something... Asking what to do.

A tear trickled from the corner of my eye. I trembled and dropped my chin to my chest.

The evening had been so wonderful. Bob Seger was singing *Mainstreet,* and my mind was drifting back to all the times I had listened to that song and dreamed of such a moment. Seger's idealized woman from the song had come to life and was lying beside me on the couch with her head on my chest, her hand stroking my arm as I played with her soft brown hair.

She had reached out for her wine glass on the coffee table, raised her head and taken a sip. She looked at me and smiled with a dreamy look on her face, parted her lips a bit, and pulled me to her. Our lips had just begun to touch when the banging began at the door.

Someone was calling that he needed help—the voice had a vaguely familiar pitch. I couldn't place it.

I looked at Callie, she shook her head. I looked back toward the front door. I sat up and shifted my weight. Callie's hand pressed down on my shoulder. Her fingertips dug into my flesh. She mouthed the word "no." The pupils of her eyes reflected the candle in the darkness of the room.

The banging continued...

"Please, help me," the voice pleaded.

I knew I had to help. It was not in my nature to ignore someone in need. I rose and eased to the door. I felt a knot in my stomach as I slid the lock back and turned the knob.

I shouldn't have.

The door burst open, hitting me in the face and slamming me to the floor. A very angry little man grabbed me by the hair and pulled me up to my knees. His strength seemed to exceed his frame many times over.

Something hard slammed into my cheek as he whipped his hand back across my face. He grabbed my hair to stop me from falling again and pressed the barrel of the pistol, whose butt had slammed into my cheek, against my left temple. He screamed for me to give up the money and that I had better not hold back on him because he knew I had money in the house.

That's when I remembered where I had heard the voice. It had an unusually high squeaky quality that cracked at times.

He lived down the block and had walked past my yard one day and asked for water. I had been chatting with Joey from next door, who was teasing me about keeping all my money stuffed in a mattress in the house or buried in the backyard.

Joey was a certified dumb ass who made stupid jokes with no basis. He knew I had no money, but his unceasing need to be funny compelled him to recycle the same four or five jokes without end or context. I never dreamed anyone would believe him.

The man was squeaking out that he wasn't playing with me and would blow my brains out if I didn't cough the money up. I was frozen in place, immobile hearing Bob Seger singing *No Man's Land*. I probably would have smiled at the irony of the timing if I could move. Seger crooned about a man whose fear kept him from making a stand. All the while I was frozen on my knees, lacking freedom like the subject of the song.

Moments ago, I was free. If only I had not opened that door. I was surprised how active my brain was despite being seemingly separated from my body, which seemed to be on vacation. I could not move and wondered if I was having a stroke.

That's when the air erupted around me. Everything seemed to simultaneously be both in slow motion and hypersonic. A spray of blood filled the air, and I had no doubt I was dying.

I wondered when sense and sensation would cease, feeling blood run down both sides of my face. I blinked hard and saw Squeaky strike the floor beside me. That's when I realized that, except for the cut on my cheek, most of the blood was not mine.

I looked towards the couch where Callie stood. The flickering candlelight highlighted the silver of the barrel in her hands. Blue smoke wafted from the end, causing a surreal blur as it drifted out into the room.

Where did that come from? I didn't know she had it. That's when I doubled over onto the floor.

I didn't stay there long,

Squeaky's lifeless stare unnerved me, so I climbed back to my knees. *What now?* I tried to ask, but nothing came out. At least I don't think anything did.

* * *

"We should just call the police. It was self-defense," Callie stormed.

"No! You *killed* him. We'll both go to prison." My eyes must have been as wide as saucers. She dropped the bath cloth she had used to clean my face and shook her head.

"What are you saying, then? What do we do? We can't just pretend he's not here."

"Uh, uh... I don't know." I waved my hands, the pitch of my voice rising to match that of Squeaky's, "I just don't know. Why did you shoot him?"

"What are you talking about?" Her eyes flashed, "He was going to *kill* you, you were there."

"What are you doing with that *thing* anyway?"

"This is crazy," Callie picked up her phone, "I'm calling the police."

"Stop!" I cried, "Those... Things... Are illegal here, even if you don't shoot anyone with it. They're going to put you away. First, you'll spend the next three years in court, then the ten after that in prison."

"What do *you* think we should do? Bury him under the floorboards? Like some Edgar Allen Poe, or Nathaniel Hawthorne shit?" Her glare scorched trails across the room as her eyes darted about.

"Callie," tears welled in my eyes. "Don't you see? This ain't some little Podunk backwater.

The 'he needed killin' defense won't work here."

This drew a sharp glare then an eye roll. "What about the gunshot? Won't the police be coming anyway?"

"People hear shots all the time around here. This is gang territory. People like us are the only ones not shooting off guns at night." I looked down at the revolver sitting on the coffee table then back to her face. "Well, people like me anyway. Couldn't you have just shot the gun out of his hands or something?"

"Honey, I'm good, but I'm not that good," she rolled her eyes. "That only works in the movies." Callie stumbled back and plopped down on the couch, bit her lower lip, then buried her face in her hands.

I looked at Squeaky on the floor. Still dead. *This problem isn't going to solve itself.*

"Well," she exhaled through her fingers. "What do we do now?" Callie looked up, pursed her lips, and cocked her head to one side.

"There's a deep lake a few miles away."

Fortunately, the man was small, I was able to force his body into an oversized metal foot-locker. Callie sat on the lid to hold it in place as I snapped the fasteners shut.

I laid cables and chains that had been sitting in my garage from the previous owners in the trunk of my car beside the footlocker. The lid barely shut.

I remember moving in and wondering what I would ever use those old metal lines for. I had nearly taken them to the dump many times, not able to imagine what use they might be.

I imagined no longer.

The chains and cables, with extra concrete blocks looped through them, would give the container more weight and prevent it from surfacing or opening once nature began to work on the old locker.

We drove out into the country and parked on a bridge overlooking a particularly deep spot in the lake. When the footlocker splashed, Callie and I traded looks. There was no turning back.

Our lives changed forever on that lonely stretch of road. I had never laid eyes on her two months before, but now the curves of her face, highlighted by the soft glow of the moon, were forever etched in my imagination.

Maybe she was right. Maybe we should have called the police and taken our chances with the system.

Over the next several days, I set about eradicating all traces of evidence from the house. Try as I might, I could not get the blood out of the carpet, so I ripped it up and laid hardwood floors.

I couldn't afford to allow anyone else into the house until it was done, so Callie and I did it ourselves in the evenings. She slept over and we fell into bed exhausted after working on the house, and curled up together.

On Saturday, I had a small dumpster brought in to dump the rolls of carpet I had been piling in the guest room. I carefully planned it, to dump the soiled carpet right in the middle of the bunch.

Several rolls lay along the bottom, and I had just dumped the bloody roll on top of them when I saw a man in a suit strolling up my walkway. A black Ford sedan was parked on the street.

"Hello." He flashed a badge. "I'm Detective Flynn." I stepped toward him, hoping to keep him away from the dumpster.

"What can I do for you, officer?"

"You seen dis man around?" Flynn handed me a wallet photo.

I glanced at it, trying to feign interest and keep any signs of recognition from showing. It was him—the man Callie had shot that night.

The angry then later lifeless features were burned into my brain. Now, I had a look at a smiling version from an old high school photo.

The version I held was that of a warm, friendly, approachable teenager, not the snarling visage who had confronted me in my entryway.

There was no doubt though, it was the same man. What had life done to him to affect such a change? That's when I realized, I didn't even know his name.

"Sorry, no." I handed it back.

"Doing a little home improvement?" Flynn leaned against the dumpster and threw a quick glance over the rim.

Dizziness threatened to overcome me. A bead of sweat ran down my temple and pooled along my collarbone.

"Yeah, it's hot out here today ain't it?"

"Uh, yeah," I quickly nodded.

"Anyways, dis guy's been missing a few days, so if you hear anyting, give me a call," Flynn pulled a business card from his pocket and held it out for me.

"Sure," I took the card and nodded.

Flynn walked back and stood by his car. He lingered by the driver's side looking up and down the street for a moment before climbing in and driving away.

I sagged against the dumpster and nearly wept.

* * *

Callie had finished her business in the city and was now three hundred miles away in her tiny town.

That night as I slept fitfully, I awoke with a start. The room had turned chilly. Footsteps thumped outside the bedroom. A shadow moved across the room and stopped at the foot of my bed.

It seemed to have no features and was darker than the rest of the room. I rubbed my eyes. It stood there for a moment then slightly leaned in toward me before pulling back and fading out.

I jumped up and ran around the house. No one else was there.

I settled in my chair in the living room and drifted off.

I continued working on the house and became obsessed with making improvements. Since that night, nothing seemed right with the place. There was a restlessness about the air. The atmosphere was often heavy.

Thankfully, I did not see the specter again, but I often heard footsteps. And once, I saw a fleeting shadow outside my door.

I began staying up late, working into the night. After finishing the floors, I moved on to the kitchen cabinets. Then, I replaced light fixtures.

I wrote several letters to Callie that I never sent. I don't know why I didn't send them. Somehow the words never seemed right. I was careful not to mention what we had done in writing. Next to that, nothing I could write to her seemed all that significant.

Late one night, I was wiring a new ceiling fan in the living room, just a few feet from the couch Callie and I had been sharing the night *it* happened.

A loud pop suddenly filled my ears, and my vision went white. A jolt racked my body. I yelped and landed on the floor as blue sparks spewed from the fan. I shook my head trying to clear my vision, watching the sparks fly.

I lay there as sparks turned into a small flame, then into a larger flame. I couldn't be sure, but I thought I caught a glimpse of a shadow in the corner of my vision. I turned my head to see it disappear into the bedroom.

The flame became a blaze.

I can't explain it, but I just lay there for a moment and began to laugh.

I briefly considered staying to see the fire from the inside—fully take in the experience. The same survival instinct I had felt *that* night finally kicked in, and I crawled into the entry-way, pausing for a moment where Callie had shot the hapless home invader.

It was now clean hardwood, but I could still see the dark stain in my mind—drenching, oozing, and soaking everything. Rising to my feet, I glanced back before walking through the door and into the night. I plopped down on the front lawn and that is where the firefighters found me, asleep.

In the light of the next day, I sat on the lawn staring at the smoldering heap that was once my home.

How temporary everything is upon this earth. A building of stone one day is a smoldering rubble the next. One day you're a big shot in your gang, or perhaps an excited new initiate looking to make your bones, the next you're residing in a footlocker at the bottom of a lake.

Fate is indeed a fickle mistress. As fickle as Callie seemed to me. I had heard nothing from her since she had left. She was gone and the pain of her absence was as much my companion as were the events of that one fateful evening.

I knew I must do something to reestablish our connection. After all, we had a link only understood by people who have been to war together.

I would find a way.

She fascinated me unlike any woman I had ever known. Nothing could change that. I knew she felt the same way. She must.

Detective Flynn sat down on the lawn beside me almost without my noticing. He gave me a quick nod and joined me in staring at the pile of charred bricks and wood. A gust of wind kicked up a wisp of dust.

Out of the corner of my eye I could see Flynn was watching me.

"Too bad about da house, huh?" I nodded and cut my eyes over, but kept my head trained forward.

"You know, I was tinkin about dis guy I been lookin for," he continued. "Funny ting how in a city like dis, somebody can just go missin without a trace."

I slowly turned my head to face him.

"Just gone... Poof! No trace." He was shaking his head, but kept a steady gaze on me, studying my eyes.

"People have all kinds of wild ideas," Flynn was grinning. "Tings like satanic cults... Even dose who tink it's some kinda alien abduction or other ridiculous bullshit. Either way, they're just as gone.

"You know what I tink?" The detective leaned in and squinted as if he were sharing a secret. "I tink they just meet up with da wrong person. Maybe somebody tougher. Maybe somebody with bad intentions. Who knows? Maybe dey even had it coming." He waved his hand dismissing the notion. "Don't make no difference to me, you see. I'm just doin a job. I don't do my job, den there's lawlessness. We can't have dat." He shook his head, "No sir, I don't have the luxury of caring who's right or wrong. I just enforce the law and I do it damn good."

I was looking closely at him now. I could feel my face slightly twitch but said nothing.

"You know how most of deese crimes get solved?" He let out a slight chuckle. "Conscience... Or pride. You see either way somebody is gonna have to get it off their chest or brag about it, eventually." He let that hang for a moment. "Sooner or later, dey always do."

Flynn yawned and stretched. "But what do I know," he continued. "Maybe the schmo did have it coming. Who's gonna miss him anyhow?" He shrugged and flipped his fingers up one by one in a counting motion. "His mother, who will swear what a good boy he was. His baby daddy he only saw once... Twice a year his whole life," he chuckled. "Oh yeah, and that circle jerk of gang bangers he run with. They'll probably miss him."

A piece of charred wood lifted off the ground and sailed several feet through the air before landing about ten feet in front of us.

"Holy jeez! Did you see dat? Musta been some kinda freak wind gust."

I nodded but kept my own counsel about the wind gust. There was something on that property that was angry and always would be. The detective's words were unsettling to more than just me, it seemed.

Flynn shook his head, "Of course given another year or two, it would be him in my jail and some other jerk-off on da slab."

Flynn grew quiet for a moment, leaned forward, and looked me square in the eyes. "You know what I would tell the unlucky bastard who done this?"

I kept still, neither shaking nor nodding my head. Just returning his stare, trying to not betray any emotion.

"I would tell the dumb yutz he's best off to just leave and never tell nobody nuttin about anyting." He punctuated his point with a quick jab of his finger into my shoulder.

I blinked twice and breathed in and out slowly for a moment. "I hope you find him," I said.

Flynn chuckled and slapped me on the shoulder as he climbed to his feet.

"I'm sure he'll turn up somewhere." Flynn winked and strolled away.

I began breathing again once he was out of the yard.

I had grown up around the corner and bought the house years ago thinking of it as an investment—a starting point which I could soon sell for a profit and move on up. With my folks gone and only a few distant members of my family left around, the house was all I had connecting me to the city.

Except for my snooty cousin who lived on the north side of town, that is. Not that he ever really stayed in contact. So, I never counted him, not for a long time. None of the family heirlooms had come my way. Nothing of real value or lasting meaning was in that house... Except the life blood of a man who likely meant to kill me.

Fire and water had cleansed that now. A smile crept onto my face like that of a man with a cancerous limb removed.

There would always be a hole, but the relief of its absence was undeniable. That's when I realized it was time to move on. I would not rebuild. I would take the insurance check and leave that as a lot for some other unlucky person to build on. That damnable shadow could haunt someone else's brand-new house.

When I returned to work after two days, it was to give my notice.

* * *

Two weeks later, I pulled up to a little cafe three hundred miles south in a town so small I was sure they counted the cows in their population numbers.

Gravel crunched under my feet in the unpaved parking lot and the door to the building squeaked as the hydraulic closer pulled it shut.

The highlights in the waves of her brown hair brought a smile to my face as I took the stool beside her at the counter.

"Hello stranger," Callie smiled. "You new in town?"

"Something like that," I tilted my head and tried to give my most suave Rhett Butler grin.

"It's good to see you," she said. The waitress came over and I ordered coffee. Once she left, Callie fixed me with that sharp gaze. "So, what are your plans?"

"I don't know. Maybe I'll stay around here." I smiled, "Find a job or something."

Callie's lips quivered in a somber half smile. "We both know that's not a good idea."

"Why not?"

"We're both safer if we're not together," she looked away from me shifting her eyes toward the grill. "One can keep a secret better than two."

I studied the curves of her face. She stared straight ahead for several seconds then turned and fixed me with her deep blue eyes.

"We would eventually betray one another..." she took my hand. "You have to know that."

"But..."

"No buts. You have to move on... Somewhere completely new. Clean slate." She let go and spanked her hands together as if knocking off dust.

"But..." My voice caught in my throat for a moment. "Where am I going to find someone like you?"

She stared at me for a moment, her lips curving upward on the left corner. "Sweetheart..." She reached out and brushed my cheek with her fingertips. "I went home with you. I didn't take you to raise."

I slowly nodded. My eyes felt moist. Callie's palm settled onto my cheek, and she leaned in and kissed me.

"You take care of yourself," she traced her fingers under my chin. "And never speak of what happened again."

I grasped her hands for a moment then pulled them to my mouth and placed a soft kiss on her knuckles.

I rose and walked through the squeaky door out into the sunlight of the young day.

The courthouse at the end of the block formed a five-point intersection.

Which road to take...

Which one, indeed.

ABOUT THE AUTHOR

J. KEITH JONES

J. KEITH JONES IS A native of Georgia who divides his time between the two Carolinas. He examines the human experience through both fiction and history in long and short form writing.

Jones is the author of several books and has had his work featured in *Georgia Magazine*, and *Gettysburg Magazine* among other journals.

You may learn more at Keith's website at www.jkeithjones.com

Facebook community: https://www.facebook.com/jkeithjoneswriting

RIPPLES

I WILL ALWAYS BE YOURS

VAL LOTZ

WHEN I WAS A TEENAGER, Grandma started calling me her girl, but it wasn't always so. My father, her son, had married an out-of-towner from back East with three kids, and she did not like it one bit.

Grandma was born and raised in dusty Colorado mining towns with dirt roads and hard people, and she wasn't prepared for her son to become an instant father. (To be fair, neither was Dad.) She didn't think the relationship would last and kept her distance, but I was a precocious and persistent child.

I loved my grandmother's home. Books seemed to line every wall, and plants populated every corner and window table. She had one plant that stood ten feet tall in its pot and had fat, smooth leaves. It looked tropical and the leaves drooped over her couch.

I sat in the corner of the couch and imagined I was part of the *Swiss Family Robinson* and had to come up with cool inventions to make life easier on the island.

When Grandma wasn't looking, I randomly pulled books off the shelves and read pieces of them. I was partial to books with dusty covers and old spines. Little did I know my imagination and love of reading would be the catalyst for our lifelong connection.

Our relationship progressed when she broke a hip, and I visited and talked to her about history or read her poems from the books with the dusty covers and cracked spines that I had perused during holidays and dinners in her home.

She had sharp blue eyes, and I could tell she was impressed that I had bypassed flashy books and the few kid books she had picked up at yard sales in favor of more intellectual pursuits. I was fascinated with Colorado history, the Gold Rush or bust, the trek of pioneers across the brutal plains, and the history of mining towns.

Her father, her husband, and my dad had all been miners. She loved telling me stories about them and the local mines. She found it endearing that I loved to read poetry and wanted to share it with her, so we spent hours talking about books, and poems, and history.

And just like that, I went from being an annoyance to a joy.

"I knew there was something special about you," she said during one of my visits.

"What do you mean?" I asked.

"You're not my flesh and blood, but you could be. You're like me. You're my girl."

The swell of pride and acceptance I felt in hearing those words still fills me to this day. I was Grandma's girl. I smiled and she smiled back. We both knew that we had a special bond.

Like all children, I grew up, moved away, and started living my life, but I always kept in touch with my grandmother. One year, I lived in the Czech Republic where I taught English. I loved sending her letters on stationery.

One of my first adventures while teaching in a small town in the Czech Republic was simply finding a place that sold stationery. I described the Czech economy in a small town as an each-sold-separately economy. When I went in search of paper, I did not find any at the grocery store or the pharmacy, the way one might in the U.S.

Upon searching my phrasebook for the word *stationery*, I looked up and found a store named after it: *Papírnické*.

She loved hearing about those simple, but in her mind, "bold" adventures.

I had visited home numerous times over the years, but in my late thirties, I returned to Colorado to visit my best friend, my parents, and my grandma. On that visit, I could see Grandma was getting older and needed help.

My parents were also getting older and were not as capable of helping. I missed my best friend, my family, and the beauty of Colorado, so I applied for jobs, flew home, packed my stuff, and moved out to Canon City, Colorado two weeks later.

When I returned, it felt like no time had passed between Grandma and me. We still talked about books, and poems, and history. We both loved old movies and watched them together.

I cut my hair short in my twenties and came out in New Orleans when I was twenty-five, and then to my parents in my late twenties. But, my father asked me to never march in a gay pride parade on TV without my top and made me promise to never come out to my grandmother. I was grateful for his acceptance and agreed.

One day, however, Grandma and I sat and watched a movie with Clark Gable. She turned to me and said, "Clark Gable was gay, you know?"

"I've heard that," I responded with arched brows, wondering where the conversation was headed.

"I wouldn't care if you were gay," she said. "You're my girl."

I looked at her and smiled. "I know that, too."

I was single in my late thirties, with a love of suits, button-down silk shirts, and short, sassy blonde hair. It wasn't much of a mystery, but I made a promise to my father. I knew my grandmother would love me whether I told her, or not.

After all, as she said, I was still her girl—until one day when I wasn't.

My grandmother was in her nineties when Alzheimer's crept in with the slants and shadows of fall's afternoon rays.

We would be watching a football game or *Wheel of Fortune* and she'd turn to me and say, "I guess I should be getting home now. Mom will be waiting for me."

I was startled when it first occurred, and like most people, I argued with her.

"This is your home, Grandma," I'd tell her, or "You're already home."

I saw her confusion and anxiety ratchet up as she looked around and saw unfamiliar or unexpected surroundings and the hour grew later.

I quickly learned I needed to change my responses.

"Oh, yes," I'd say. "I told your mom I'd have you home by six PM. Is that okay, or would you like to leave now?"

She'd apprehensively look at her watch, but she would usually settle down for a little while before asking the same question again.

Sometimes, I had to load her in the car and drive her around until we came back to the dirt road to her home and I'd say, "Look, Grandma, there's your proud pink house. We're home."

"This is my home?"

"It is. Don't you remember us painting it pink? And look, your flowers lining the walk. This is definitely your home."

"I guess it is," she'd say.

It was clear she struggled to reconcile the timelines of her life.

I moved in with my grandmother to help her daily. I was fortunate to work for an online school and had remote days so I could work from home and be available for Grandma, but it was over those days that everything changed.

I made us dinner one night. As we sat at the kitchen table eating pork chops, green beans, and mac and cheese, she turned to me and earnestly said, "You know, I think it's nice that you're this handsome young man and you clean and you cook for me, but we moved in together kind of fast, didn't we?"

I tried to contain my bewilderment and take it in stride. I gave a thoughtful look and shrugged.

"Oh, no, honey." I took her hand in mine. "When it's right, it's right. We're supposed to be together," I said with conviction.

She thought about it for a moment and then nodded. She smiled and squeezed my hand. "You're right. It's right."

I won't lie, I felt a little pervy and like I should apologize to my father and deceased grandfather at first, but as the days wore on it was clear I was no longer her girl, I was grateful she still saw me as someone she trusted and was safe with.

One time, I had to pick her up from the hospital after a fall. I walked into her hospital room and gently rubbed her shoulder to wake her. Her face lit up as if I were the sunrise to end all her sundown experiences.

"Hey, are you ready to get out of here?" I conspiratorially asked.

"I'd go anywhere with you," she said. "You're my guy."

"You know it," I said with a wink.

I was able to keep her in her home for a while. I'd wake her up and help her put her teeth in, put her hearing aids in, and then I'd put her glasses on and tuck the frames over and behind her ears.

"Where's Mom?"

"Oh, you know your mom," I'd say. "She's already up and about, gathering eggs and other chores. Want to help me make breakfast?"

"We'd better," she'd say with the eye roll that comes naturally to every teenage girl.

I smiled and helped her to the kitchen table where she would drink coffee while I fixed breakfast.

We maintained a routine for a while, but unfortunately, her earlier fall weakened one of her legs. She continued to struggle and fall at home. We finally had to put her in an assisted living facility.

It was hard to visit her there. I felt immense guilt for not being able to take care of her at home, so I did not go as often as I would've liked. There were times I went when she was anxious and fearful, which only increased my guilt. There was little I could do to assuage her panic. Other times I would go and find her sitting alone, eating her meal in the dining room.

She would look up and say, "Where the hell have you been?"

"Working too much, but I'm here now."

"Well it's about time," she'd say, with a mischievous smile.

We'd sit together and talk. In her mind, she was still a young woman living in Cripple Creek, Colorado. Her mom was still alive, but her father had already passed on. He'd worked in a coal mine and died of pneumonia when she was only ten. She was a daddy's girl.

One day, I met her in her room when the sun was just going down—trapping her somewhere along the timeline of her life. The curtains to her window were pulled back and there was a sleek red *Camaro* out front.

"Did you bring your hot rod for me?" she asked, nodding at the *Camaro*.

"Oh, no," I said, blushing. I owned a *Kia*. "That's not mine. I have Dad's car today."

"Do you ever think back to high school and how maybe you were the one who got away?" she asked, while biting her bottom lip.

That was new information for me. She never mentioned she might have had an interest in anyone in high school. Despite all our time together, she was still full of mysteries and stories to tell.

"Me? I was a fool to let *you* get away."

"We should have taken a drive in that car of yours," she said, wistfully looking out at the *Camaro*.

"Yes, we should have. I think about that all the time," I told her. "We would have been happy together."

"You're here now," she said, turning back to me.

"I'm here now," I agreed, and she smiled.

"You're still my guy," she said, reaching for my hand.

"I will always be yours," I told her, closing my fingers over hers.

She smiled, and we both turned away, lost in our thoughts.

We quietly sat together while the sun slid behind the mountains, leeching the red, gold, and orange hues into shadows and shades of greens, greys, and navy blues.

I turned to her and could see the confusion stealing over her again as she released my hand and retreated into herself.

But I was certain—I was *her girl.* I was *her guy* somewhere in the passages of her mind.

And I will always love you, I thought.

And, I still do.

ABOUT THE AUTHOR

VAL LOTZ

VAL LOTZ HAS LIVED IN numerous places but considers Colorado her home. She started writing stories for her friends when she was nine after her mom bought her a *Brother* typewriter at a yard sale.

She published her first story, *We Danced in the Sun*, in *The Maverick Press* when she was a Junior in high school.

Val always thought she would become the next Judy Blume or Robert Cormier, but life as an educator at high school and college levels is more demanding than she thought, but even more rewarding than she imagined.

She still writes and aspires to publish young adult novels, but she also loves to write lesbian romantic comedies in a similar vein to the works of Robin Alexander, without the Southern flare. If Val's work resonates positively with you, please reach out via email at: val@brainstormlearning.org

RIPPLES

What's in a Name?

Regina d' Scriptura

WHO MAKES AN IMPRESSION ON us so much that our lives are changed in so many ways? Our parents? Our siblings? Our friends or colleagues? Strangers?

You decide.

The young woman walked down the street. Her head lowered as she passed the construction site. The workers turned toward her as she approached. They whistled and cat-called, as they did every afternoon. Her face grew hot. She tried to ignore their taunts. She told herself it was all in good fun—they were being complimentary. But their words didn't feel like compliments. In fact, she felt dirty and wrapped her jacket around her torso, attempting to cover her breasts. Once again, she found herself wishing they weren't so big.

I must love my body, she reminded herself. *I must accept all of me if I ever want anyone else to accept all of me.* She repeated in her

head the mantra she'd heard all her adult life...
Which up to that point was about ten years.

"Most girls would know how to handle this
situation... But then again, most girls have
at least been on one date by the time they're
twenty-eight," she mumbled as she continued
toward her home. With each step, the rude com-
ments faded, and her posture straightened.

She checked the mailbox in front of her small
home.

Empty.

She opened the gate of the white picket fence
and admired the blooming lilacs which edged
the short staircase to her veranda. She deeply
inhaled, allowing their soft fragrance to envelope and relax her.

Rodger waited for her.

"Hi, sweet one." She reached down to pet her
black cat and scritched behind his ears. "I'll
get you food as soon as I get my slippers—"

The ring of her phone cut her promise short.

"Hello?" She placed her work satchel and
purse on the counter and changed ears. "Oh,
hi Mom. What's up?" Rodger wrapped his body
around her legs and purred.

"Mmmhmmm," she said. She opened the cup-
board and pulled out Rodger's food. "But why
would I want to do that, Mom? That would make
me hugely uncomfortable."

Rodger's food created a melody as it fell from the box to the bowl. He abandoned her legs and sniffed his food. He looked up at her and meowed.

She covered her phone's mouthpiece. "Rodger, you like this one. I promise." Then, speaking into her phone, she said, "Mom. Maaawwwm. MOM! You know I despise blind dates."

She made her way through the living room. "I don't care if he is your new boyfriend's son and is visiting from out of state. Please don't make me. *Please.*"

She flopped down on her bed and lay back. "Ugh! Fine! You win. As always. I'll meet him. I'll make him feel welcome and show him around the town. When and where?" She sat up and grabbed the notepad and pen she kept on her nightstand. She scribbled down information.

"Tonight? Really, Mom? At seven? That only gives me about forty-five minutes to get ready and walk there." She sighed. "Fine. Whatever... Wait! Mom! What's his—" Her words were cut off by the click of the receiver.

"...name?"

Rodger sauntered into her bedroom and jumped onto her bed. He settled in next to her, licked his paws, and waited to be petted.

"Don't get comfy, Rodg. I'm *'going on a date'*. My first one, because my mom apparently wants time alone with her boyfriend." Her head tilted back, and with eyes closed, she sighed again. "I didn't even get the experience of being asked." She plugged her phone in to charge and went to her closet. "What to wear? What to wear?"

* * *

The Tipsy Turvy was dimly lit when she maneuvered through the waiting crowd to the hostess station.

"Just one?" The perky blonde rose up on her toes as if preparing to lead a cheer.

She felt her cheeks burn but held her composure. "No, I'm meeting a friend. A boy. I mean, a man. A guy."

"Is your friend here yet?

"Uh... No? I don't know. I'm a bit early, so—"

"There's no wait at the bar. You can wait there for him and have a drink while you wait?" The hostess turned to the next in line.

The restaurant wasn't busy, but a line *was* forming. She decided sitting at the bar was a good idea. She could look around without much notice and maybe figure out who her date was. Her mom had mentioned he was a computer geek like her.

The barstool was a tall chair with padded seat and back. She chose the furthest stool, which looked out over the restaurant and comfortably placed her in the corner with her back to the wall. She put her purse on the chair beside her.

She reached in to check her phone. It wasn't there.

"Crap." In her mind's eye, she saw the phone tethered to its charging jack on her nightstand. "Double crap."

"Can I get you something?" The bartender polished a glass while looking at her breasts.

She resisted the urge to lean down to make eye contact with him. "Yes, please. Can I have a mojito?"

When the bartender answered, she was unsure if he spoke to her left boob or her right one. "We're out of—"

"Of mint. I get it. In that case, I guess I'll take a beer—whatever you have on draft. In a cold glass, please."

"Can I see your ID?" He placed the over-polished glass on the counter and his eyes finally looked into hers as he held out his hand.

She handed him her driver's license. He looked it over, handed it back and, without a word, turned and walked away.

Two or more people sat around the occupied tables. She was certain she'd beat him there, so all she had to do was watch the door for a geeky loser like herself to walk through them.

* * *

She was on her second draft beer when she decided he was a no-show. She looked at her watch. It was fifteen to eight. *Forty-five minutes is long enough to wait for Mom's boyfriend's son.* She raised her hand to get the bartender's attention.

At that same moment, a man walked through the door and waved back. He headed her direction. Her heart skipped a beat and stopped at the same time. Part of her wished he'd not showed, and another part of her felt relieved he'd not stood her up, even though she didn't know the guy from Adam.

He didn't look like much of a geek, just a shy guy—a very nice-looking shy guy. She didn't think he was gorgeous, but he definitely had looks you'd never get tired of. *Besides*, she thought, *if he were any more buff, I'd have to compete with the gym.* She smiled at the thought of being competition for a man's attention.

"Well, you have a beautiful smile," he said, as he reached out his hand to shake hers. "I'm Chris."

"Oh, my goodness. That's my name, but with a 'K'." The female Kris laughed, blushed at his compliment, and noticed, all at the same time, his eyes remained on hers.

"Have you been waiting long, for uh...?"

"No," she lied.

He stood next to her as if he didn't quite know what to do or say. His hands kind of floated while he searched for words. His fingers finally found purchase in his front pockets, and he shyly smiled.

"Uh... Do you mind?" He gestured toward the stool which held her purse.

"Oh! Yes, please..." She placed her purse on the bar. "Sorry. Please, sit."

He picked up the long-abandoned menu. "You must be hungry. Shall we order?"

Dinner went smoothly. Kris forgot her uneasiness as they fell into conversation. She found him fascinating. She enjoyed his opinion, as well as his eagerness to hear her thoughts without interrupting. They spoke little of personal matters, sticking to subjects more generic in nature. What book did he find most fascinating and could he recommend a good podcast. What type of movie did she enjoy, and would she like to go to the movies with him sometime.

Not once did his eyes devour her breasts. That alone gave her permission to relax and enjoy his company.

"I have had an enjoyable evening, Kris-with-a-K, but it's getting late, and I'm pretty sure you have work in the morning. Shall we call it a night?"

Kris surprised herself by feeling disappointed. She glanced at her watch. It was just past midnight. She looked around the restaurant and saw the tables were empty. A few patrons remained at the bar, but the employees were cleaning for the evening.

"Oh. Oh, yeah. I guess we should."

"Can I walk you to your car?"

"I walked. It's such a nice night and our town is really, well, as you can see it's quite small. Just driving here, I'll bet you saw it all. No need for me to show you around." Kris giggled. The beer made her a tad light-headed. Or maybe it was his cologne. Or his smile?

His face wore a puzzled expression. "Can I give you a lift, then?"

"Oh, no. That's okay. I only live a short distance away."

"Are you sure?" He seemed concerned.

"Yeah. Yes. I'm sure."

"Can I at least walk you home?"

"Uh... Sure. I guess."

The night was clear and warm. A chinook breeze tussled Kris's hair as they walked side by side up the street, talking. His hand occasionally brushed hers, and she felt a tingle shoot up her arm. When they got to her house, she turned to him.

"This is me."

Chris looked at the small but beautifully kept home. "Is that a Victorian?"

"Yep. Turn of the century. The last one, that is. Not this one." She giggled. "I restored most of it. I hired an electrician and plumber, of course, but the rest of the work I did."

"Wow! I am impressed. Brains and handy. You are something else. I am so glad I got to finally meet you, Kris." He held out his hand. "Can we do this again sometime?"

"Sure. Yeah. I'd like that." His grip was firm, but gentle.

He reached into his pocket and handed her a small rectangle. "It's my card. Call me? Or text me with yours? And that way I can call you. Your call... So to speak." His smile nearly melted Kris's heart.

Kris looked at the print—it was too dark to read. "Yes. Yes, I will. Thank you. This night has been an unexpected pleasure." She slipped his card into her purse.

Chris squeezed her arm, smiled, and turned. She watched him walk to the end of her street. He turned back and waved and then disappeared into the darkness. Kris felt his warm energy leave hers. She smiled and headed up her walkway and into her house.

"Meow?"

"It was perfect, Rodger. I can't wait to get to know him better." Kris sat on her bed, pulled Rodger onto her lap, and stroked his fur. "If Mom's boyfriend is anything like his son, he's okay with m—"

The vibration of her phone caught her attention. It was her sister, Meagan.

"Hey, Sis. What's up? A little late to be calling, don't you think?"

* * *

Chris walked down the dark street toward his car. With every step his anxiety rose. Had he just messed up the best thing that ever happened to him?

He recognized her as soon as she walked in. He knew her walk—the graceful way she held herself amid the cat-calling. She didn't recognize him in the restaurant, and she didn't notice when he left. When he saw her still sitting alone, he impulsively reentered. He had meant to be forthcoming. She expected, and thought, he was someone else.

As he walked, he thought he'd never see her again. Especially after she found out. He felt his heart break a little.

* * *

"What do you mean, Mom's trying to get a hold of me? Is she okay?" Kris stood, knocking Rodger from his comfortable position. He mewed in disgust and repositioned himself on her good pillow. "Well, yeah. I did have dinner with—wait, what? Slow down. Who's Danny?"

* * *

Chris looked up from his paperwork. He had been staring at it without comprehension. His mind replayed the events of the evening before. The foreman stood at Chris's desk.

"What do you need, Bob?"

"That new tile that came in. It don't match what we got. Darrel wants to put it up anyways, but I told him that'd never sail. I don't like him, boss. He's cuttin' corners left an right.

And he thinks he outranks me." Bob poked his stubby finger at his chest. "Ya gotta do somethin' or I'm walkin'." Bob nodded his head as if in agreement, placed his hands on his hips, and waited.

"Again. We've been through this, Bob. I'm not your boss. I'm the project manager. You need to take your beef up with Jake."

Chris watched Bob's face grow red from the neck up. His mouth worked for words.

Chris pushed his chair back and stood. "Tell you what." Chris walked around and placed his hand on Bob's shoulder. "I need a break. Let's go seek out some good coffee and find Jake. We'll sort this out together."

Bob's shoulder relaxed under Chris's hand.

As they walked through the job site, Chris heard Darrel whistle. "Hey, beautiful. Why don't you walk them titties this way?" Chris heard the others laughing and whistling.

"Darrel! I warned you. You clean it up, or you pack it up. Your choice." Chris stood more than a hundred yards from Darrel, but Darrel had no trouble hearing Chris. He whipped around to face Chris.

"Aw, com'on, boss. We's just havin' fun. She gots them tig bitties." Darrel mimicked holding two large melons, crossed his eyes, and licked his lips while his hips provocatively gyrated.

Chris strode up to Darrel and put his nose within inches of Darrel's.

* * *

Kris plainly heard his first warning, but she couldn't hear what Chris said next.

When she'd heard Chris's voice, she involuntarily looked up and stopped walking. She watched Darrel's cocky stance quiver and melt into submission.

Chris turned his head her way. She quickly dropped hers and hurried down the street toward work. Her heart pounded.

When she sat at her desk, she pulled his card from her purse. She'd nearly thrown it away after realizing the prank he'd pulled. She worked and worried his card so much, it no longer looked crisp and new.

CHRIS WEINBERG, PROJECT MANAGER

ALBEIT CONSTRUCTION

"Why did you do it?" she asked the card.

"Sorry, hun. I didn't hear you." A head popped up over the top of Kris's cubicle. "What d'ya say?"

"Oh, sorry, Dawn. Was talking to myself."

Dawn's entire face lit up and her eyes sparkled. She had piled her long, black curly hair into a messy bun, held together with a pair of small purple knitting needles. "Gotta watch that, deary. Soon you won't be needing any man... Keeping your own council, and all."

Dawn's wide smile faded as Kris's face broke into silent tears.

"Oh, sweetie." Dawn rushed around the drab-cloth partition to Kris's side. "What's wrong?" She wrapped her ample arms around Kris, who succumbed to sobs and allowed Dawn's kindness to undo her.

"Come on. Let's get you to the breakroom. I'm super glad I got here early today." Dawn emphasized her words with a snug hug and led Kris to privacy.

While Kris blew her nose multiple times and relayed events of the prior twelve hours in detail, Dawn listened, nodding when appropriate and occasionally tsk-tsking. When her tale was told, Kris felt spent and exhausted.

"Did you get any sleep last night?"

"No." Tears again welled up in Kris's eyes.

"Okay, sweetie." Dawn paused for more than a few seconds. "Can I be blunt?"

Kris nodded.

"Alright. We've worked together for, what? Eight years? I think I know you well enough to say this..."

* * *

Chris's heart dropped in his chest when he realized the girl who had turned away and rushed down the street was his Kris.

Can this day get any worse? "Darrel, I mean it. You're done or we're done. Do I make myself clear?"

Darrel's bowed head nodded.

"Come on, Bob. There are three coffees with our names on them."

Bob had to nearly run to stay with Chris. "Three?" he managed, through his huffs and puffs.

"Yeah. One for Jake. Keep up."

* * *

Darrel was not used to being chastised, especially not in front of others. "Fucker's gonna git his," he said under his breath as he stormed away. "You are so right, Chris-tow-fer. You *are* done here."

He turned the corner to the stairway, taking two, sometimes three steps at a time as he rose out of sight.

* * *

Bob opened the door to the site shack. "Boss... I mean, Chris. Someone's here to see you."

"Send him in."

"Uh... She... Won't come on site." Bob kicked at the door frame.

She? Chris's heart stuck in his throat. "Uh... Okay. Where?"

Could it be her? No. Why would it be her? Who could it be, though? Martha from accounting. But... Martha always comes on site.

"Chris?" Bob's face wore a puzzled look. "Did you hear me?"

"Um, yeah... No. Sorry." Chris felt his face grow hot and he cleared his throat. "What did you say? I was, uh... My mind was on... The books." Chris indicated the paperwork on his desk.

"I said, she's south-west of the portas, just inside the boundary. You can't miss her."

"Did she say what she wanted?"

"Nope. We've been through this, Chris. I'm not your secretary." Bob winked as he walked out, leaving the door wide open.

* * *

Kris's hands were stuffed into her pants' pockets. Her feet shifted weight from left to right to left again. *Why is this taking so long. I'm going to lose my courage... Come on. Come on. Where are yo—*

Her thoughts were cut off when she saw Chris emerge from the site shack. Confusion played on his face. She watched as he noticed her and hesitated for a split second before continuing forward.

She admired his strides, the way he held his shoulders back and his head straight. The plaid work shirt, blue jeans, and work boots stirred a pleasant feeling inside her and she smiled. Her heart beat faster the closer he got.

A flash caught her attention, and she looked to its source. At the top of the structure, a figure stood next to a pile of beams. The man had a piece of rebar in his hands and was levering it under a few of the top beams.

Chris is walking right under that. "NO!"

Chris continued walking, his smile growing with each step closer. They were still a few hundred feet apart.

Kris held out her hand. "Wait! Stop!"

He waved at her.

He can't hear me with all the noise.

Her heart pounded. She sprinted toward him. She heard the beams give way. She watched as Chris's smile turn to confusion. He stopped directly under the falling beams. She felt as if she were running through mud. Everything seemed to move in slow motion.

She looked up as the beams bore down.

She solidly hit Chris's chest. The force catapulted him backward and knocked him down. She landed on her stomach and instinctively covered her head with her hands.

Please, God, was the last thing she thought before the beams struck.

* * *

She awoke in a daze. She couldn't move. Her eyes wouldn't obey her command to open.

Where am I?

She tried to take a deep breath through her nose. *Ouch!* The air smelled antiseptic and cold. Multiple soft beeping sounds awakened her ears.

She struggled to remember what had happened.

His face. His three-day stubble beard. His kind eyes. His smile. The way he laughs. The way he walks... His rugged work shirt and pants... He... He was walking toward me... Smiling...

Kris's eyes shot open and filled with tears.

"Meagan! I think she's waking up." *A man's voice.* A voice she didn't recognize.

She felt a hand take hers.

"Kris? Kris, can you hear me? You've been in an accident. You're in the hospital. You've had to have surgery. There were some complications. Kris?" *Meagan's voice.*

"Mom. Kris is awake." *Meagan's voice again.*

Kris's eyes wouldn't focus. Lights and shadows filled her vision.

"Oh, Kris. Oh my God, Kris." Then sobs. *Mom's voice.*

"Mom! That *is not* helpful." *Meagan's voice. She thinks she's whispering.*

Kris heard a door open and close. She tried to take a deep breath and another wave of pain stopped her.

"You have some broken ribs, sis. Try not to do that." *Meagan's voice.*

"Should we get a nurse? Can't they give her more pain meds?" *The man's voice.*

Kris heard a call beep. A feminine voice over the intercom spoke, "Nurse's station. What do you need?"

"Can we get some pain meds?" *Meagan's voice.*

"Be right in." *Intercom.*

Kris blinked and tears flowed down the sides of her face. She cleared her throat and pain engulfed her.

"You had a breathing tube down your throat for the better part of a week. That pain will cease." *Meagan's voice.* Kris felt the hand she thought was Meagan's squeeze hers. She attempted to squeeze back and succeeded.

"Nice, little sis. I felt that." Kris felt a cool hand touch her cheek. She leaned into it. She felt her tears being wiped away, which caused more tears to flow.

"Shhhh, sis. It'll be okay. I'm here. Mom's here. Danny's here..."

Danny? Who's Danny? Where is Chris? Why isn't Chris there? Panic rose in her chest. She heard the beeping of the hospital monitor increase. Her chest heaved with uncried sobs, causing more pain.

The door opened. Footsteps grew closer. She felt her limbs being moved, pressed, checked. A warm tingling started mid-arm and gently moved throughout her body. She felt warm and relaxed. Just before she drifted, she heard the female voice from the intercom, "That should do it. She'll be out for a while. You may want to get someth..."

The rest of the nurse's spoken words wafted into a hall of warped echoes then faded as Kris fell into a dreamless state of being and unbeing.

* * *

"Chris. Where are you?" She screamed through the darkness.

"Shhhhh... I'm here." Meagan's voice brought her out of her dream. Kris opened her eyes and was able to focus on the hospital room ceiling. Images came into view. Her mind slowly acknowledged them, one by one.

Meagan was seated next to the hospital bed, leaning forward and holding her hand. Kris gave it a squeeze. Meagan squeezed back and smiled.

"Hi, Punkin."

"You..." Kris cleared her throat and tried again. "Haven't. Called. Me. That..."

"I know. Since you were little." Meagan wiped a tear away. "I know I'm older, but you've always been my hero."

"Ele...ven... Years..."

"Way to rub it in." Meagan laughed. Kris tried to smile.

A male face appeared beside Meagan's, wearing a concerned look. "Hey, I'm Danny. We were supposed to go on a date the other night, but my car broke down. Your mom said you wouldn't answer your phone. I am so sorry."

So, that's Danny. "S'okay."

Meagan gently placed her hand on Danny's shoulder.

Great. They're bonding while I'm lying here after... Why am I lying here? "Why... Am I... Here?"

"You, kiddo, walked onto a construction site for some unknown reason and got yourself clobbered by falling debris. You've been in a coma for about... What day is it, Danny?" Meagan's voice belied her attempt at upbeat banter.

"Eleven days, I think. No, twelve... Maybe?"

"You were rushed here, put in an induced coma for a brain bleed, and immediately operated on. We don't know how bad your other injuries are yet, but time will tell. Your job is to heal."

"Where is... How is... Chris?"

"Kris?" Meagan shot a desperate look at Danny. "Punkin... You *are* Kris. Do you remember me? Meagan?"

Exhaustion filled Kris's soul. She nodded at Meagan. "Yes. Tired." Kris closed her eyes and tried not to cry. She soon fell into a fitful, but blessed sleep.

When she awoke, Kris felt a presence in the room. She opened her eyes and looked upon a man dressed in white standing bedside. *An angel? Chris? Did you die?*

As her eyes focused, she noticed a stethoscope around his neck and a name badge: DR. SMITHJOY.

"Hi, Kris. I'm Dr. Smithjoy. How are we feeling today?"

"Okay...ish."

"You gave us quite a scare. The beam hit you on your back just from the point of your head, here..." Smithjoy indicated a point on the lower back of his skull. "...just missing your hands, straight down your spine, That's what kept you from being compromised or paralyzed. You did, however, have extensive brain trauma and a severely cracked skull."

Smithjoy picked up Kris's arm. "Press against me, please."

Kris complied to the best of her ability.

"That's to be expected." He pulled a pin light from his lab-coat pocket and examined her eyes. Kris winced at the brightness. "Good. Good. There's that, then."

The doctor pulled the computer keyboard close. He spoke while he made notes in her chart. "All-in-all, you look very well for being most nearly dead. We're moving you out of ICU this afternoon. You'll remain on the brain monitor for a few more days. If you continue to press on as well as you have been, we'll have you out by next week." He finished his notes, pushed the keyboard back to its original spot, and smiled. "How does that sound?"

Kris's eyes welled up. "Is the... The other guy... Okay?"

Concern swiftly crossed the doctor's face, then he maintained composure. "You'll have moments of confusion. That's to be expected from a head injury. I'll put the order in to move you. Maybe tomorrow we can start you on clear liquids." He squeezed Kris's arm. "I'll check in on you tomorrow."

"Wait..." Too late. The doctor disappeared behind the solid wooden door. Just before it clicked shut, it opened up. Kris looked toward it with anticipation.

"Hey, sis." Meagan's face appeared. Danny's right beside hers. "Can we come in?"

"Yes."

"Good news, right? We spoke with the doctor before he came to talk with you. Out of ICU this afternoon. That's amazing." Meagan was giddy with happiness. Danny took Meagan's hand and pressed it to his lips. She lovingly gazed at him.

"How—?" Kris's question died on her lips. But Meagan knew what her sister was asking.

"We told them he was my husband. Mom was concerned about me being alone with you, so she sent Danny to sit with me. With *us*."

"Oh." Kris didn't know why, but she wanted to be alone. Seeing her sister happy was nice, but them together like that turned the knife in her heart a little bit. "Tired."

"Okay... We'll, um... I guess we'll go. Can I bring you anything?"

"No." Kris closed her eyes. She waited until the footsteps faded and the door clicked behind them before she allowed her eyes to open. She stared at the ceiling, trying hard to not think of Chris with a 'C'.

She didn't speak when the nurses moved her to the general ward. She didn't respond when Meagan said goodbye and that she and Danny would be back in the morning.

RIPPLES

When the morning sun hit her window, she opened her eyes and decided to "get busy living or get busy dying" ...something she had heard in a movie once upon a time. Her hand searched for the bed remote and slowly raised the bed to a seated position.

Sitting in a chair at the end of the room was Chris.

"Are you... A ghost?"

A short laugh escaped his lips. "Of all the things I thought you'd say, that wasn't one of them." He stood and walked to her bedside. He took her hand in his. "How are you feeling?"

"Better. Now, that... You're... Not dead."

"I'm not dead."

"What... Happened?"

"Well, after you knocked me on my butt, my hardhat flew off, my head hit a brick and literally knocked me out. When I came to, the EMTs had already sent you to the hospital and they were working on me. Tough head." He knocked on his temple. "Not much damage. Just a slight concussion. They didn't know... Or didn't tell me much about your injuries.

"Darrel... The guy who gave you grief almost every day... Ran after you were hit. They caught up with him in Middletown. The site's cameras have it all recorded. He's being charged with attempted murder. Two counts.

"Anyway, that's why I'm here. I am so sorry to have put you in danger. The beams were meant for me. You should not have been there. I am grateful you saved my life, but I will forever feel guilty for you nearly being killed." Chris lowered his head.

"I'm... Sorry." Tears welled in Kris's eyes. "Thank you... For coming."

"Why *were* you there, Kris?"

"Dawn. My friend. She told me... A kind man... Is difficult... To find... And... To not lose him... When I find... Him." Tears flowed down Kris's face. She felt as if she'd lost Chris before she even got to know him.

Chris wiped away her tears. "You're not going to lose me anytime soon."

"Why did it... Take you... So long... To get... Here?"

"I didn't know your last name, Kris with a 'K'."

RIPPLES

ABOUT THE AUTHOR

REGINA D' SCRIPTURA

REGINA D' SCRIPTURA HOLDS DEGREES in Writing, Sociology, and Graphic & Commercial Arts. She's been featured on radio shows, invited to speak at schools, and has participated in conference panel discussions and presentations.

Regina lives in Wyoming with her wiener dog, Rodger. They camp, hike, and enjoy nature whenever they can. Life inspires Regina in both her writing and her art.

Regina's short stories and articles have been published in many quarterly magazines. This is her first submission to an anthology.

RIPPLES

THE PASSION

GARY B. ZELINSKI

PART 1. ALL THE ROMANCE ANYONE NEEDS

AFTER YEARS OF A LIFELESS marriage, there was only one fantasy left. Making love on a secluded beach. Living in Iowa presented some obstacles, but they could wait. Time was all they had left.

Clifford and Brenda grew up in Iowa, on the side of the state that's cold in the winter and hot and humid in the summer—the side just like the other side. The side was flat with nothing but feed corn and soybean fields as far as the eye could see.

He was from Dubuque, she from Des Moines. Any closer, and they'd have been related. Clifford grew up tall for his age; then he settled into just being tall. His constitution was solid, and his nervous energy belied his ability to eat twenty or more *Snickers* bars in one sitting, a highlight of the county fair. Now in his early forties, he's six foot four and carries his one-hundred-twenty-seven pounds like the weather vane planted in every Iowa yard.

Brenda wasn't homely as a child. Or, so her mother says. Not fat but far from slim, yet of steady stock—one capable of plowing six acres before the horse was out of the barn. With her *Brenda Lee* raised-heel shoes she got for her seventeenth birthday, she stood five foot, four.

Early in their marriage, they told people destiny brought them together, and God blessed their holy Iowa union. The facts remain. When they were sixteen, it wasn't so much fate as a consequence of the competition.

Brenda won first prize at the county fair that year. Clifford entered the contest as a joke and the peer pressure of the other boys. Brenda beat all takers that year in the strong arm, best man arm-wrestling contest. Clifford came in second and was her trophy.

A few decades after a quick wrist and bulging biceps brought their love together, they were alone. They lived together, but Brenda and Clifford had long since grown apart—drifting in their marriage like the blowing Iowa snow. Secretly longing for the passion buried in the mound of snow piled high and left by the plow.

The Iowa snowplow of loneliness covered their mailbox of love.

Clifford's search history was full of long-dormant passion. He was careful to delete it. They shared a single out-of-date computer and almost everything else. He knew they shared too much when he caught her cleaning the sink drain with his toothbrush.

Their marriage seemed over. Little did he know, she had the passion as well. Smoldering, not buried deep, but hidden, right below her ample bosom. Mostly she ignored it. Ignoring her passion like she tried to ignore the bloating she often felt.

One too many Iowa biscuits, she thought.

Then, one day she saw it—his history file still there, a careless mistake. Though she'd never admit it, she was curious. She had the passion, too.

STAR-CROSSED LOVERS. A SECLUDED BEACH. COME TO JAMAICA, the ad said. COME TO THE LAND OF ENCHANTMENT, LAPPING WAVES ON A SANDY BEACH—RUM DRINKS WITH FRUIT.

Just then, she felt it surfacing from under her ample bosom. The bloating took over again. The moment was ruined. Not completely, but temporarily on hold. For now, she had more pressing desires.

Working at the feed store didn't leave much money after the bills were paid. He managed to save some. He hid it from her. She'd just blow it. Pay the gas bill on time for once. Or maybe buy that toaster oven she'd been eyeing down at *Markel's Five 'n Dime*. Yeah, he hid his money, just like his passion, or so he thought.

She hid her money, too. Twenty-plus years of buying groceries and picking up the slack for his lack of ambition. An extra nickel here or there. She was the saver of the family. Cutting hair, doing makeup. She had her own business. It didn't bring in much, but as Brenda said, "A nickel here, a nickel there..."

What she really liked and the thing she did most often was read *the cards*. At the time, tarot cards were frowned upon in Iowa. Many so-called parlors were raided by the local police. Raided due to the suspicion of drugs and other such non-Iowa things. Couldn't have that in our community.

But you couldn't stop Iowa women from wanting her to read their cards. And so it goes, for every local gal who had their hair done, two, sometimes three, wanted to know what the cards had to say. Some came back week after a fruitless week. Truth was, the cards always said the same thing. She was an expert at knowing what the local Iowa women wanted to hear.

"Will he leave me?"

"When will he leave me?"

"Why won't he leave me?"

But there was another question all these women wanted to know: *"When the hell am I going to get out of Iowa?"*

Next, Part 2 - The Passion Builds...

* * *

PART 2 – THE PASSION BUILDS...

And so, he in his world, her in hers. Alone, yet together. The Iowa winters can be cold. An Iowa home without love is like an unlit stove— full of potential. But potential and the internet can't keep the Iowa wind from blowing and chilling your bones.

Secretly and ever so slowly, their passion was building. Building like the foundation of an Amish barn. One brick, or dare I say it, one click at a time.

The winter came and went, and the crops were planted, then harvested. Once more, the cycle was completed. Knee-high by the fourth of July was the norm for Iowa corn, but the summer and autumn would see no growth in their love.

Their secret passion lay dormant like hordes of buried cicadas. Maybe seven years, maybe eleven, before the sticky wings of their love would emerge like thousands of pupae yearning to mate.

That winter, there would be no Kevin Costner in her field of dreams. ...or, so she thought. For him, half-forgotten images of their youth filled his dreams. They met at the state fair twenty long years ago. The arm-wrestling contest was a lark—a dare from friends. It would seal their fate, but that was the following year. They first met the season prior.

She had just won second prize for the heaviest sow. He was delivering hay when their eyes met. The job paid seven dollars a day but more than enough to buy her that corn dog and funnel cake she had always cherished. While the eight-hundred-pound pig dined on Fred Quiglinger's finest alfalfa, the two lovers, mere children that they were, snuck away for a stolen kiss in the night under Iowa stars.

But working at the feed store left him little time to daydream. Chickens needed corn, and the hay needed delivering. Promotions were tough over the years, but still, he was proud to be driving the delivery truck. Well, driving when Charlie Walkensworth was out sick, or on a weekend, and there was a feedlot emergency.

Charlie was a big man, close to three hundred pounds. His left eye seemed stuck in neutral, not cross-eyed, or dead. His left eye seemed to float and roam about like that big carp in the feed store's fishpond. He also reeked of tobacco juice. A bad habit he'd picked up in the third grade when the pressure of failing citizenship sent him into therapy at the local Lutheran Church. But still, as the owner's son, Big Chuck had seniority.

It was eventually bound to happen. The history file was still there, nothing on TV, and he was tired of sitting in the delivery truck's hot seat, playing second fiddle to reeking Chuck.

She was bored, too. The cards were cloudy and didn't speak. The cards were silent and bleak, just like the winters in Iowa—silent, grey, and overcast.

She had pain in her stomach all day, and now she was tired. Tired of feeling like that errant single sock in the damp misty hamper of life.

Did she mention it first? Or was it him? No, never him. He'd be too embarrassed. She just didn't care anymore.

"Well? Well, are we?"

"Sure. Why not? What *did* you say?"

"I said, are we ever going to go?"

"Go where?"

"You very well know what I'm talking about. Don't change the subject."

"What subject?"

"Really, Clifford. I really don't know you anymore."

"Oh, for crying out loud. I had a tough day."

"A hard day, Clifford? A hard day smelling Chuck's farts? Sitting on your ass? Yeah, you had a bad day."

The conversation could have gone on like this for hours. They often did. But for some reason, maybe riding in the cab of that old run-down delivery truck, there was a weakness in the marriage forcefield. The kind of protection that grows around a marriage gone sour—a wall that insulates one from the torment of the other.

"Well, fine. What the hell? We don't need a new riding mower this summer anyway. Besides, Jerry and Sheryl's cow eats most of our grass."

"See? It's always about you, Clifford. It's always about you."

"I was going to buy the mower for you," he started to say but didn't. "Fine, let's go to Jamaica."

"What the hell." *Does it have to be with you?* She thought.

Next, Part 3 -Wings of Passion

* * *

3. Wings of Passion

The plane ride was miserable.

First, you had to drive to Dubuque, catch the shuttle to Des Moines, and then onward to Minneapolis. Minneapolis was where everyone from the Midwest went to fly out of the Midwest. Their 'economy minus' tickets offered five inches less legroom than that of the overhead bins, but heck, they already blew most of their savings on the charges for all that extra luggage.

No self-respecting Iowan would ever take a trip in the winter, even to Jamaica, without two or three pairs of flannel underwear.

The lack of legroom forced Clifford to contort his six-foot-four frame into a fetal position.

When the snacks came, there was no hope of lowering the tray. The four croutons and a half-ounce of squeeze cheese rested comfortably on his knees. He was miserable, but he'd promised himself to give their marriage one last chance. Passion will do that.

Meanwhile, Brenda had her own problems. While she had plenty of legroom, when the farmer in the seat in front of her tilted back, her ample bosoms were pressed up towards her chin.

She gained temporary relief when she lowered her own tray. Relief because it forced the farmer's seat to invert forward. Her breasts then comfortably rested on the tray table, but her arms were hopelessly pinned at her sides.

Opening, then eating the package of croutons with her teeth was no problem. Opening and sucking the squeeze cheese out of the vacuum-sealed plastic was, again, no problem. The little cup of diet cola turned out to be a problem.

Given the tight quarters, Brenda couldn't lift her arms. A diet cola was firmly wedged between her two generous mounds. No straw. The cola was just an inch or two out of reach. Turbulence ensured everything was in constant motion.

Her breasts jiggled up and down while the diet cola sloshed side to side. She tried to reach the lip of the plastic cup with her teeth. No luck. She tried freeing one arm. No luck. In desperation to get just one sip, she forced her head down like she was back at the county fair bobbing for apples. A forceful plunge into the small cup of cola.

Maybe a bit too forceful.

The diet cola went everywhere. While she got a few sips of drink, most of the syrup went up her nose. Before she could raise her head, she sneezed. The sneeze was loud, causing her to violently exhale, breaking the top two buttons of her blouse.

The sneeze woke the sleeping infant in the row behind and set him to wailing. It woke Clifford as well.

Looking over and seeing Brenda's unbridled breasts, he said, "I can't wait to get to Jamaica, either."

They landed on time in Minneapolis. The flights from Minnesota to Kingston and on to Ocho Rios were uneventful but long, thus ensuring our Iowa passengers were tired, sore, and hungry. They finally arrived late at night.

Next, Part 4 - The Lapping Waves of Passion.

* * *

PART 4 – THE LAPPING WAVES OF PASSION

The budget resort, which looked promising in the online brochures, looked more like the *Travel Lodge* on I-80 than a Caribbean getaway. While available and plentiful, it didn't provide food.

The brochure said: EVERY ROOM A SUITE! Upon inspection, it technically qualified as a suite because there was a half wall separating the toilet from the two twin beds.

Clifford and Brenda, too tired to talk, found a different twin bed and fell fast asleep.

Mornings came early in Iowa but not so much in Jamaica. Sleeping in slightly past seven, they had to wait until ten before the diner across from the motel opened for breakfast.

The diner would be their eating place morning, noon, and night. The diner served chicken. Eggs for breakfast, chicken fried steak for lunch, and jerk chicken for dinner.

To give it a homier feel, before they're your food, the chickens became your friends. Chickens roamed the streets, lived in the motel lobby, and even shared your beach umbrella.

Clifford took to naming the chickens, which didn't sit well with Brenda.

"Maybe you should read their cards."

"The future doesn't look bright," Brenda replied.

It was the first joke they'd shared in twenty years.

"Why'd the chicken cross the road?"

"Stop."

The beach was a few steps from their room, but it took a few more hours before they could get there.

Brenda unpacked the various oils, ointments, and lotions she'd carefully packed.

Tender Iowa skin burns easily in the hot Jamaican sun. Clifford's arms and neck were as dark as the immigrants and farm laborers who took all the good Iowa jobs—arms a golden brown that hid the truth. His pale, anemic bloodless skin had never seen daylight. Dracula couldn't draw blood from his pasty white frame. Lucky for him, his Iowa underwear covered most of his lanky frame.

Brenda was a different problem altogether.

Brenda had one of those all-year-long tans. The tanning booth in their basement saw to that. For Iowa women who were willing to pay, the tanning booth was a perk after their new bouffant hairdo, courtesy of *Brenda's Cut and Curl*.

Brenda's real problem was her bathing suit. Most tops were too small, and most bottoms too big. No fewer than seven different combinations in various sizes were needed to fit Brenda's unique Iowa frame.

Finally greased up, lathered up, and prodded into their respective attire, they hit the beach.

The small beach bar was a local kid on a bicycle with a cooler. But, the rum drinks were cold. Clifford and Brenda got their own sampling of fruit and a different colored umbrella for stirring. They might have been in heaven.

The air was warm, and just as advertised. The waves gently lapped at their feet. The couple, after so many years, finally had something to say.

And walk and talk they did.

First separated, but then slowly, their fingers met. Not quite holding hands, their fingers seemed to glide along one another's. Not that holding hands was out of the question. Being free from Iowa norms and customs, they were finally able to show public affection so sternly frowned upon on the streets of Cedar Rapids.

Caressing fingers was excitement enough—it would have to do. Holding hands was impossible due to the amount of ointment and grease they'd applied. Just when one of them moved in for the grab, the other's hand shot out like the piglet neither of them could tackle at the fair.

Drinks were long gone. They'd walked for hours along the deserted sands and clear waters of their new Caribbean hideaway. Finding their spot, they sat for a rest and...

If the problems began when they sat, they only got worse when they laid down—being so heavily greased caused a myriad of problems.

First, both became coated in sand. If their hand touched the sand, it spread. When they looked at their behinds, it was like looking at a coating of flour on raw chicken.

Problems continued when they each snuck a peek beneath their respective swimming attire.

Clifford found sand in places he was hoping to keep free. Brenda found sand in places... Well, let's just say Brenda found a lot of sand.

Realizing any more displays of affection would only lead to chafing, the likes of which were akin to the rubbing and bruising they got back in high school when they hid and canoodled in Uncle Milton's grain elevator. Nobody wanted that memory to return.

Returning to their room well after ten in the evening, three hours past their usual bedtime, they showered. It took a long time to wash the sand from all those hidden places.

Finally clean and ready for bed, Clifford put on his last clean pair of Iowa underwear.

"Maybe Iowa's not that bad," he said.

"Not if I can be there with you," she said.

The sun sets early during Iowa winters. Brenda and Clifford don't mind.

RIPPLES

About the Author

Gary B. Zelinski

Gary B. Zelinski decided to write professionally in 2020 when his father passed away due to complications from dementia. It's not hereditary, but memories fade even for the best of us.

His memoir, *Aim High, a Love Story,* and his book about service members buried at Arlington National Cemetery, *A Walk Among Heroes*, will be published in 2024.

When you meet someone at age twelve, fall in love, and spend the next fifty years together, it's hard to know where one person starts and the other ends. Gary retired from the USAF after twenty-two years. His bride, Lillian, raised two delightful children and rose through the ranks to become a senior vice president for a *Fortune 500* tech company.

Gary and Lillian have three self-published books on Amazon. They are a collection of stories from their travels, first in a sailboat to the

RIPPLES

Bahamas and next in a camper to the National Parks and Alaska.

Everyone has a website and blog.

Here's his: https://bound-for-glory.com

Made in United States
Orlando, FL
09 January 2025